He g...
knuckles whitened. Look after
Nina... If anyone deserves a holiday...

He glanced at Nina, now immersed in her more personal letter. She had other envelopes scattered around her. Letters with destinations written on the front. Gran's dream itinerary?

Reaching the end of her letter, Nina grabbed a tissue from the box he'd had the foresight to place on the table, dried her eyes and blew her nose.

He handed back the letter and tapped a finger to his. "Looks like we're going to the Mediterranean, then."

She froze. "You too?"

"She asked me to be present at the scattering of her ashes."

Nina folded her arms. Her lack of enthusiasm stung. He pulled in a slow breath. "I wish she'd told me," he croaked out. "I'd have taken her on that cruise in a heartbeat." He leaned forward, tapping a finger to the table. "Let me arrange everything. It's the least I can do under the circumstances. And then let's give my grandmother the last hurrah she always dreamed of, yes?"

After the briefest of hesitations, she nodded.

Dear Reader,

Back in August 2024, I asked my newsletter subscribers what their favorite tropes were. The winning trope was marriage of convenience. Next in line, though, was friends to lovers, which started me thinking... My debut book was a friends-to-lovers tale, and while I've written a couple more over the years, it's been a long time since I've penned one. The more I thought about it, though, the more I wanted to write another friends-to-lovers romance. And that's how Nina and Blake's story was born.

Nina and Blake have been best friends since they were four years old, and while they've kept in touch over the years, they haven't actually clapped eyes on each other in a decade. When they finally do, sparks of a most disconcerting nature start to fly. Throw in the fact that Nina is furious with Blake for "reasons," and that his grandmother's last request has them embarking on a Mediterranean cruise together, and it's a recipe for tons of delicious conflict and lots of soul-searching.

I loved watching this pair reassess everything they thought they knew about each other and find their way back to one another. I hope you love it too.

Hugs,

Michelle

TEMPTED BY
HER BEST FRIEND
BILLIONAIRE

MICHELLE DOUGLAS

ROMANCE

If you purchased this book without a cover you should be aware that this book is stolen property. It was reported as "unsold and destroyed" to the publisher, and neither the author nor the publisher has received any payment for this "stripped book."

Harlequin®
ROMANCE

ISBN-13: 978-1-335-47049-2

Recycling programs for this product may not exist in your area.

Tempted by Her Best Friend Billionaire

Copyright © 2025 by Michelle Douglas

All rights reserved. No part of this book may be used or reproduced in any manner whatsoever without written permission.

Without limiting the author's and publisher's exclusive rights, any unauthorized use of this publication to train generative artificial intelligence (AI) technologies is expressly prohibited.

This is a work of fiction. Names, characters, places and incidents are either the product of the author's imagination or are used fictitiously. Any resemblance to actual persons, living or dead, businesses, companies, events or locales is entirely coincidental.

For questions and comments about the quality of this book, please contact us at CustomerService@Harlequin.com.

TM and ® are trademarks of Harlequin Enterprises ULC.

Harlequin Enterprises ULC
22 Adelaide St. West, 41st Floor
Toronto, Ontario M5H 4E3, Canada
www.Harlequin.com

Printed in U.S.A.

Michelle Douglas has been writing for Harlequin since 2007 and believes she has the best job in the world. She lives in a leafy suburb of Newcastle, on Australia's east coast, with her own romantic hero, a house full of dust and books, and an eclectic collection of '60s and '70s vinyl. She loves to hear from readers and can be contacted via her website, michelle-douglas.com.

Books by Michelle Douglas

Harlequin Romance

One Summer in Italy

Unbuttoning the Tuscan Tycoon
Cinderella's Secret Fling

One Year to Wed

Claiming His Billion-Dollar Bride

Summer Escapes

The Venice Reunion Arrangement

Escape with Her Greek Tycoon
Wedding Date in Malaysia
Reclusive Millionaire's Mistletoe Miracle
Waking Up Married to the Billionaire
Tempted by Her Greek Island Bodyguard
Secret Fling with the Billionaire

Visit the Author Profile page
at Harlequin.com for more titles.

To Greg, who went above and beyond
when I was neck-deep in this book, always there
with an encouraging word, chocolate or glass of red
whenever I needed them. Sending you
all the London and dinosaur emojis.

Praise for
Michelle Douglas

"Michelle Douglas writes the most beautiful stories,
with heroes and heroines who are real and so
easy to get to know and love.... This is a moving
and wonderful story that left me feeling fabulous....
I do highly recommend this one, Ms. Douglas has
never disappointed me with her stories."
—*Goodreads* on
Redemption of the Maverick Millionaire

CHAPTER ONE

BLAKE'S LUXURY SEDAN all but limped into Callenbrook, his home town in rural Victoria. The home town he hadn't visited in over a decade. If he'd had his way, it would've been another decade before he'd returned.

His nose curled and his scowl deepened. His grandmother's voice sounded through him. *Be careful the wind doesn't change.*

An old wives' tale, Gran.

What he wouldn't give, though, to hear her voice one last time.

Don't think about that now. Unclenching his fingers from around the steering wheel, he tapped them against it instead and considered travelling the extra thirty minutes into Bendigo and getting his tyre fixed there. Ever since he was fifteen years old he'd dubbed Callenbrook 'Red Neck Falls', and the fewer people he had to engage with here, the better.

With a growl, he turned and headed into the town centre, pulled in at the auto mechanic's workshop. Joey Lockyer came strolling out from the inside. As soon as Blake emerged from the tinted-windowed interior, though, Joey looked as if he'd like to turn around and head back inside. With a deep breath, he set his shoulders and kept moving in Blake's direction. Blake and Joey had never had any issues with each other. Hopefully they wouldn't now either.

Joey pointed to one of the front wheels.

'Run flats,' Blake said.

Why the hell hadn't he specified his rental car have an actual spare tyre that he could change himself rather than run flats he'd have to get replaced by somebody else if they were punctured?

'We've one of those in stock. You're lucky. I've a few jobs in front of you, though.'

'What time you want me to come back and collect it?'

He waited for Joey to shrug and say, 'Never.' Waited for him to tell Blake to take his business elsewhere.

'I'll be hard-pressed to get it done this afternoon. Tomorrow morning would be more convenient. It'll be ready by eight.'

Convenient for whom? Though, as the funeral wasn't until ten, he couldn't claim it as an inconvenience to himself. He was grounded here until after the reading of his grandmother's will.

He tossed Joey the keys. 'Want me to pay up front?'

Joey huffed out what might've been a laugh. 'Tomorrow will be fine, Blake. Don't forget, any time after eight.'

Pulling his duffel bag from the boot, Blake slung it over his shoulder and, with a nod, set off on the six-block walk to his grandmother's duplex. Before he was out of earshot he heard one of Joey's workers say, 'Who was that?'

'Blake Carlisle. Iris Day's grandson.'

'Finally here in the flesh, then?'

Blake's nose curled. Man, he hated this place.

Eight minutes later, Blake stood out the front of his grandmother's house. He stared, unable to force his legs forward to open the gate. Even though he knew curtains would be twitching at the windows in the neighbours' houses.

He glanced briefly at the house next door, the duplex that shared a wall with his grandmother's, and moistened his lips. Nina hadn't taken his phone calls since February, hadn't answered his texts. *Damn it.* The one thing he needed to fix while he was here was *that*.

His gaze return to Gran's. A decade. While he'd seen his grandmother more regularly than that, he hadn't been home in ten years. And nothing had changed.

You've changed.

And your grandmother *is dead.*

The gate, the garden, the house, all blurred. His grandmother was no longer with them. *That* was a change too big to comprehend. As soon as her funeral was over, though, and her estate settled, nothing would make him step foot back in Callenbrook again. *Nothing.*

You going inside or are you going to start howling on the front lawn?

His therapist would probably advise him to go ahead and howl, would tell him it was cathartic. The neighbours would love it.

Forcing his legs forward, he pulled out the spare key he hadn't used in a decade and he let himself inside. Closing the door, he didn't howl even though nobody could see him, but, dumping his duffel bag to the floor, he sagged back, the door reassuringly solid at his back.

The place was wrong. As if without Gran inside it, it made no sense. He really could've sat on the floor then and bawled his eyes out. Instead he did as Gran would've expected—he opened the curtains and then the windows, and took himself off for a shower.

Showered and unpacked—not that he'd packed much as he didn't expect to be in Callenbrook for more than a few days—he ambled into the kitchen and found a fresh loaf of bread on the counter, milk, vegetables and a steak in the refrigerator along with a six-pack of beer. And a few cans of the lemonade his grandmother had favoured.

Nina? Glancing at their connecting wall, he realised he had no idea where she now worked or what time she'd be home. For the last decade Nina had been her mother's full-time carer, but Johanna had died back in February. And he hadn't made it home for the funeral.

Even if she wanted to avoid him, even if she refused to forgive him, he and Nina still needed to talk.

His gut churned; bile burned his throat. He shouldn't have left it so long to come back. He should've returned as soon as he was able.

A familiar band tightened about his chest, making it cramp, and his breathing grew hard and laboured. Closing his eyes, he focused on counting his breaths, regulating them, until the grip loosened. Hooking out a chair at the kitchen table, he pulled out his phone and played a game of Tetris. When he was done, his breathing had almost returned to normal, his mind calmer again.

He made a sandwich even though he wasn't hungry because low blood-sugar levels wouldn't help. And he wasn't losing the plot. Not now.

He didn't hear Nina come home, nor did he hear her move about next door. He rapped out their old signal on the kitchen wall a couple of times, but received nothing in reply. Not even a curt two-knock 'Not now' that had been their standard language.

Yeah, a decade ago.

Maybe so, but she wouldn't have forgotten.

At a little after five he couldn't stand it any longer. Grabbing a lemonade from the fridge, he headed outside to the back veranda, stopping short when he saw Nina sitting in a vinyl armchair in a startling shade of electric blue at her end of the veranda, staring out at her garden. Dragging in a breath, he forced his legs towards her, stopping at the knee-high iron railing that separated the two properties. 'I didn't think you were home.'

She didn't turn to look at him, but continued to stare out at her garden. He glanced at it too and his brows shot up. Nina had loved green things and gardening ever since Gran had put a trowel in her hand as a five-year-old and set her up with her own little plot.

He'd known she'd extended her garden, but this was *amazing*! Native trees and shrubs wound among raised garden beds that he knew would be filled with vegetables. The effect was an odd combination of wild and ordered.

'The garden is looking great.' He sat in the matching chair on his side of the railing, his heart beating too hard. 'You didn't hear my knock on the wall?'

'Am I supposed to come running whenever you knock?'

Right. Wrong opening. He should've said something like, 'Isn't this awful?' or 'How are you holding up?' because she'd loved his grandmother every bit as much as he had.

He ached to reach across and hug her, kiss her cheek, but the frosty eyebrow she'd briefly raised had warned him not to try it. His stomach hollowed out. He concentrated on his breathing and stared at the garden on his grandmother's side of the fence.

Nina had obviously taken over Gran's garden too—the native plants and shrubs irresistible to the birds who made a cacophony of sound in the dusk of the late August afternoon—but the rose garden his grandmother had so loved still proudly stood at its centre. Staring at it now made him ache and throb. 'You didn't hear me arrive?'

'I heard you were back in town before you left Joey's workshop.'

He shook his head. *This town.* Was that when she'd ducked across with those few groceries? Was that *her* dinner in his refrigerator? She might be giving him the cold shoulder, but she'd cared enough to make sure he had something to eat.

'You didn't think to come on over?'

'What for? You're a grown-up, aren't you? Besides, I was too busy getting over my shock that you'd actually turned up.' She raised her glass in his direction in a mock toast.

He went as cold as the ice that clinked in her glass. 'You didn't think I would?' Had she honestly thought he'd stay away and leave her to deal with everything?

'Showing up *isn't* what you do.'

Silently he swore. And swore. 'Look, Nina, about your mum's funeral...'

That eyebrow rose again when he hesitated. 'Go on. My mum's funeral…?'

When he didn't she gave a mirthless laugh. 'My mother, as in the woman you called Auntie Jo? The woman who took you under her wing and was a second mother to you because your own parents were miserable excuses for human beings? *That's* the woman you're referring to?'

'Nina, I…' But how to explain when he could barely explain it to himself.

'You didn't come back home once in ten years to see her. Not once. And you knew that, unlike your grandmother, she couldn't travel.'

For the last seven years he'd treated his grand-mother to an annual European holiday—so he could see her at least once a year and make sure she was doing okay. He'd have done the same for Auntie Jo and Nina. Jo's illness, though, had made that impossible.

He hated Callenbrook with the fire of a thousand suns. He'd never wanted to return to the godfor-saken place. Nina had always told him she under-stood.

Until February. When she'd stopped talking to him altogether.

Fact was he *had* tried to come home for the fu-neral. His hands clenched at the memory. He'd made it as far as Singapore airport before the pain in his chest and the drumming in his head had overpowered him. The shortness of his breath. The struggle for air. The way his left arm had tingled before going numb.

He'd collapsed, too dizzy and weak to communicate, unable to tell anyone what was wrong with him. A part of him had watched from afar as the cabin crew had called for an ambulance and he'd been raced to hospital. He'd thought he'd die before they arrived. A heart attack at thirty. Rare but not unheard of.

Except it hadn't been a heart attack. It had been a panic attack.

Prior to experiencing one for himself first-hand, he'd had no real idea what a panic attack involved. He hadn't known the symptoms could be so severe. He hadn't realised how debilitating they could be. He'd still been intent on getting the next flight to Australia, but no sooner had he verbalised that thought to the doctor than he'd found himself in the grip of another panic attack. Apparently telling yourself to snap out of it, that you were strong and successful and had overcome adversity before, didn't make an iota of difference. Panic attacks didn't care how wealthy you were, or how intelligent or successful or competent.

It had rocked him to his marrow. He'd never wanted to experience another one as long as he lived.

By the time the doctor had discharged him from hospital, it'd been too late to get to Callenbrook in time for the funeral. So he'd texted Nina that he'd had a work emergency so she wouldn't worry when he didn't turn up in Callenbrook, had grabbed the next flight back to London and had sought the professional help the doctor in Singapore had urged him to seek. He'd had therapy, had slowly worked through his issues, hence the reason he was here in the flesh now—and relatively coherent. But actually verbalising all of that...

Closing his eyes, he swallowed and prayed to God his voice would work. 'None of that means I didn't care.' He and Jo had spoken regularly on the phone, they'd video-conferenced every couple of months. She'd known how much he'd loved her.

'Actions speak louder than words, Blake.'

She crossed one remarkably shapely leg over the other and he found himself frowning. Nina didn't have *shapely legs*. She just had...legs.

'Luckily for them both, Mum and Granny Day continued to believe in you until the end.'

His heart jackhammered in his chest. 'But... you don't?' She was supposed to *know* him. *Really* know him. She was the only person left on this earth who did. She *had* to know there was a good reason why he hadn't made it back for the funeral.

Pursing her lips, she glared at her garden and shook her head. Just once. But it hit him like a sucker punch.

'You needn't think that means they weren't hurt when you never came home either, or weren't made sad by the fact that they never had a chance to say a proper goodbye.'

She thought him heartless. She thought he'd turned his back on them. Before the guilt and regret, the grief, could blanket him in complete and utter inertia her words hit him. *They hadn't had the chance to say goodbye.*

'Gran's passing *wasn't* a surprise?' On the quiet of the late afternoon air, his words sounded like gunshots. He'd been told his grandmother had died of heart failure.

Nina's eyes flashed, 'Hell, Blake, she received a cancer diagnosis back in January.'

January! But… 'She never said a word!'

Arms folded over a surprisingly generous chest. *Not* that he was looking. 'I believe she asked you to come home for her eightieth birthday in April. That she made it clear to you how much that would mean to her.'

She had. Which was when he'd finally confided in her about his panic attacks. He'd had several while in therapy—all connected with the thought of having to one day return to Callenbrook. As soon as she'd found out, Gran had backed off, hadn't wanted to put more pressure on him. She'd ordered him to focus on his therapy and to get better. *You should've told me, Gran.*

It was all he could do not to drop his head to his hands and weep. He should've worked harder, should've returned sooner. 'I was taking her to Uluru next month.'

'That was never going to happen. Though she did think she'd still be here. Except...' Nina's voice broke and her hand shook, making the ice in her glass tinkle. He knew her grief would be fresh and raw too, but at least she'd had a chance to say goodbye.

'What the hell...?' He rounded on her. 'Why didn't *you* tell me?'

She tossed her not quite blonde hair over her shoulder, hard brown eyes glaring into his. 'And what difference would that have made?'

Derision stretched through her eyes—something he'd been used to seeing in the faces of the townsfolk of Callenbrook, but had never seen in hers before. It robbed him of the power of speech. She thought that badly of him?

Of course she did. As far as she was concerned, he'd let down the two women who had given him a measure of stability when he was growing up, had given his hungry heart all the love it had craved. And why would she think differently? She didn't know the truth.

But she knows you...

Not any more. And apparently he didn't deserve the benefit of the doubt.

So tell her, then.

A familiar band of resistance tightened about him. He knew he shouldn't feel embarrassed or ashamed. Or weak. But he did. As his therapist pointed out, he was a work in progress.

'Besides, she asked me not to.' One slim shoulder lifted, and with a jolt he realised she'd lost weight since he'd last seen her.

It's been ten years.

Yeah, but Nina had always been slim, and now she was downright skinny. He swiped suddenly damp palms down his jeans. 'Thank you for stocking the fridge and getting in the essentials.'

'It's the least Iris would've expected of me. I've no intention of letting her down. But understand this, Blake, I did it for her, not for you.'

She rose and he blinked, because while Nina might've lost weight, she had *curves*. She must've had them ten years ago. She'd been nineteen when he'd left, but...

He shook himself. What the hell was he doing? 'Can I persuade you to join me for dinner?'

'No.'

The swift refusal had his head rocking back.

Shapely legs made for her back door. 'We need to talk, Nina.'

She glanced back, that frosty eyebrow doing its thing. 'About?'

'The funeral?'

'It's all been taken care of.'

'But—'

'Iris knew exactly what she wanted, had plenty of time to plan it, and that's what's happening tomorrow. I'm not letting you mess with her final wishes.'

He stood then too. 'I want to say a few words at the funeral.'

'There'll be an opportunity for anyone who wants to speak to do so.'

And then Nina was gone and for the first time in his sorry life, Blake felt utterly alone. Breathing in through his nose and out through his mouth, he started ticking off his list of threes—three things he could see, three things he could hear, three things he could smell.

When the darkness had receded from the edge of his vision, he nodded. *Right*. Before he left this godforsaken town, the one thing he was going to accomplish was making things right with Nina again.

Nina glared at the blue-sprigged wallpaper on the kitchen walls. Clenching her hands, she dragged in a breath.

You were too hard on him.

Too hard? He'd deserved all that and more! She'd thought Blake was a friend—her *best* friend. She'd thought he'd be there for whenever she needed him. She'd thought—

But she'd been wrong, and the pain of that still threatened to crush her. She couldn't explain it, but during the worst of her mother's illness, and at the beginning of Iris's, the thought that she had Blake's friendship to fall back on—the solidity of it—had given her comfort, had kept her strong. To know that when she needed him, she'd only had to call…

Finding out that had been a lie had gutted her.

Even so, she'd planned to act very differently when they finally came face to face. She'd planned on being polite—icily polite—to treat him like a stranger. But one look at him as he'd emerged from Iris's back door had forced the air from her lungs in a hot rush, and she'd become a giant burning ache with a huge side serving of tossed anger. That icily polite facade had liquefied in a single eyeblink.

The boy she'd known ten years ago would never have put work and money above people. The man he was now didn't deserve her consideration, and he certainly didn't deserve her generosity. He didn't deserve her warmth or the relief of sharing his grief with her. He didn't deserve an open-armed welcome or—

He loved his grandmother.

Pulling in a steadying breath, she nodded. He had. He'd cared about her mother too. And her. Just…not enough. Story of her damn life where men were concerned. They couldn't be relied upon. First her father and now Blake.

She glared harder at the wallpaper. Her mother had loved it. Maybe it was the memory of her mother, but she found herself swinging around and stalking back out to the veranda. But she kept one foot planted firmly inside her own kitchen.

'You and I will go to the service together tomorrow. It'll look odd otherwise.'

He sat eerily still in that ludicrous electric-blue armchair, as if afraid any movement would send her scuttling away again. 'Okay.'

'I want to get to the church two minutes before ten. And we'll go straight in without talking to anyone. And we're sitting in the front pew. Got it?'

'Got it.' He shifted the smallest amount. 'Driving or walking?'

'Driving. Will your fancy car be ready by then?'

He nodded.

'Then we'll take that. The tinted windows might be welcome.'

He lifted his hands. 'How on earth do you know my hire car has tinted windows?'

The same way she knew its make and model, that it was a classic navy blue, and when it came to navigational and safety features it had all the bells and whistles. It also boasted a multitude of reversing and parking cameras. The way half the men of the town talked, that darn car could damn well near drive itself. She didn't say any of that, just raised an eyebrow.

'The Callenbrook grapevine.'

He rubbed a hand over his face. She couldn't help but notice the tired lines fanning out from his eyes and his pallor. He looked done in. She did her best to stop her chest from clenching or…anything.

'Nina?'

In the twilight, shadows had gathered beneath the veranda and she couldn't make out the blue of his eyes. The intensity of his gaze, though, had a pulse inside her thrumming to life. Resentment, she told herself. 'What?' She might've snapped the word out a bit too curtly. His lips twitched a fraction, and that didn't improve her temper either.

'Thank you.'

She hitched up her chin. 'I'm not doing this for you. I'm—'

'You're doing it for Gran. I know. That's what I'm thanking you for.'

Shaking her head, she went back inside the house and closed the door behind her. Very firmly. Fact was, a part of her was doing it for him too— because of what the town had done to him as a fifteen-year-old. It'd been ugly and unfair, and she wasn't going to let that happen again. Not a chance.

Nina and Blake sat side-by-side in the front pew of the church that Iris Day had diligently attended for most of her eighty years. The church was so packed that people stood in all the available space at the sides and back of the room and in the foyer—every pew crowded except for the front one, which had been left vacant in deference to her and Blake. Until Nina rose and grabbed Iris's six closest friends and insisted they join them.

And yet it was Blake she was aware of, sitting with that same eerie stillness he had the previous afternoon. And Blake she missed like a hole inside her.

If the world and their relationship had been the way she'd thought it, she'd be sitting here holding tightly to his hand and taking comfort from his presence. Instead of mourning one person she felt as if she was mourning two—as if a double grief had taken up residence inside her heart. A heart still sore from the loss of her mother.

Pushing all of that to one side, she stood and gave the eulogy. 'Iris told me that she wanted today to be a celebration of her life and *not a misery fest*. I hope that I can do her justice.' She spoke of Iris's life and listed her many accomplishments, she shared special memories, making the assembled crowd laugh, dab their eyes, and nod.

Folding up the sheets of paper on which she'd printed out the eulogy, Nina stared out at the assembled congregation. 'Iris and I weren't bound by blood, but we were bound by something even stronger—love. She was my Granny Day. I'm going to miss her every single day, but I have so many memories to hold close and find comfort in, and I'm so very grateful to have had her in my life.'

She couldn't look at anyone as she made her way back to her seat, afraid she'd burst into ugly sobs if she caught so much as a single sympathetic eye. Florence patted her hand and murmured, 'Well done, Nina. Iris would've been proud of you.'

Everything blurred. Beside her, Blake remained preternaturally still.

'If anyone would now like to say a few words about Iris, share their memories, then I'd like to invite you to come forward now and—'

Pastor Peg didn't have a chance to finish what she was saying before the six women to Nina's left all bounced to their feet and marched up to the front of the church. 'As girls, we used to call ourselves the Seven Deadly Sins,' Enid started. 'Sorry, Pastor Peg, it was just our little joke. And it probably won't come as a shock to anyone here that Iris was Lust.'

Nina choked. *What on earth...?*

'She had such a lust for life, you see?'

Nina let out a breath and relaxed a fraction. Blake did too.

'And a lust for goodness too, which is why it was such a shock to us that she had such a nasty, conniving little minx for a daughter.'

Nina slapped a hand over her mouth to strangle a laugh. *Oh, God!*

Luckily, Enid swiftly moved on to an account of the many antics they all used to get up to and had the church in stitches. Blake, though, remained stony-faced throughout it all. The old Blake would've appreciated the dig at his mother.

Old Blake is long gone.

After the six remaining Deadly Sins had taken their seats again, eight more people made their way to the front, one after the other, to individually share a memory or reveal the impact Iris had on their lives. Iris had been a much-loved member of the Callenbrook community. And while a part of Nina reveled in all of it—because this was *exactly* what Iris had wanted—another part of her waited on tenterhooks for Blake to rise to his feet and say a few heartfelt words.

What would he say? Could he redeem himself? Even if he failed, she wanted him to try.

Despite his declaration of the previous evening, though, he made no move to stand and face the congregation. Instead the knuckles on his hands turned whiter and whiter as he clenched his hands harder and harder and his head and spine bent. She could hear the breaths sawing in and out of him.

Without giving herself time to think, she reached across and laid a hand over his, squeezed it. He gripped it like a lifeline, and then, as if aware he might be holding on too tight and hurting her, his grip slowly loosened and his shoulders lost some of their tension and his head came back up.

But he didn't rise to his feet. He didn't get up and pay public homage to his grandmother. When Pastor Peg motioned for them to sing the final hymn, Nina reclaimed her hand, disappointment wrestling with pity inside her.

Refreshments were served in the adjoining hall. Nina was swamped with well-wishers along with the gossips eager to pry from her whatever titbits they could about Blake. Not that she was giving anything away. The Deadly Sins carried Blake off to a table and, safe in the knowledge that he'd be protected while he was with them, she did her best to banish him from her mind.

This was supposed to be a celebration, and she did her best to be jolly and enjoy the anecdotes and recollections, but... In truth, she'd never felt less like celebrating.

Slipping outside, she sidled around to the back of the hall and moved across to lean against the jacaranda that would soon be in full bloom, to sip her tea and catch her breath.

'Holding up all right?'

She turned to find Robbie McAllister scuffling the toe of his rarely used dress shoes in the dirt. Poor Robbie. He was twenty-one and as awkward as they came. He'd be mortified if she burst into tears.

She could almost hear Iris's voice in her head: *His mother brought him up right, but the father...*

'Yeah, Robbie, just needed a breather. How about you?'

He shrugged. 'I really liked Mrs Day. She was a nice lady. I'll miss working on her car.'

'Fibber. I swear that little Honda of hers was being held together by duct tape and string.'

He grinned. 'It was all right.' His smile faded. 'How can you stand it? Being near him—the grandson? He didn't come near her in years and—'

'I'm guessing that's coming from your father,' she broke in with a raised eyebrow. She knew how much imagined injuries and resentments could snowball out of control in this town, and she wasn't letting that happen now. Not a chance. 'And, Robbie, we both know what a sterling judge of character he is.'

Robbie had the grace to wince. 'I suppose, but…'

'Iris didn't tell Blake she had cancer and was dying.'

The younger man's jaw dropped.

'As far as Blake knew, he was taking her to Uluru on a holiday next month.'

'No way,' he breathed.

'That's the thing, Robbie. You can't always tell from the outside what's going on in other people's lives—you can't see what's really happening or know what the real truth is. None of us should be so quick to judge. Iris taught me that.' She fixed him with her sternest glare, but deep inside she started to squirm. Wasn't that exactly what she'd done too? She'd been awfully quick to judge when Blake hadn't shown up to her mother's funeral. Maybe something had happened she didn't know about?

If that's the case, why hasn't he told you?

Exactly! She folded her arms, hitched up her chin. 'If you want to do Iris Day proud, you'll remember that too.'

He nodded, and then huffed out a laugh. 'You

know, you look kinda hot when you get all bossy like that, Nina.'

'*Robbie!*'

He sobered again. 'Is what you just told me a secret?'

He probably wouldn't breathe a word of it to anyone if she asked him not to, but movement at the side of the church hall a few feet away caught her attention. *Blake*. Had he overheard her conversation with Robbie?

Glaring at her, Blake folded his arms and gave a swift hard shake of his head. *Very private and confidential* was the silent message he sent in response to Robbie's question. Yep, looked as if he'd heard the lot. Ignoring him, she glanced back at Robbie. 'Not a secret, no. Just the truth.'

Robbie ambled off and Blake stalked across to her. 'Why the hell did you go and tell him that?'

'Why the hell does it matter?'

A hand slashed through the air. 'Because my life is none of these people's business, that's why.'

'But Iris's life is, and was—in the same way she considered their business hers. And no matter how much you hate it, her and your lives intersect.'

His head rocked back. 'I don't hate *that*. I love that our lives intersected.'

Could've fooled her! 'Where your and Iris's lives intersected, though, is the bit everyone feels is their business.'

'Well, they're wrong, and—'

'Stop being an idiot,' she hissed.

He blinked.

She pointed a shaking finger at his chest, and then pulled her hand away, frowning, when she realised what a very nice chest it was. Grief. It was just grief. It did strange things to people.

'Why am I an *idiot*?'

He bit the words out and she tried to gather her scattered wits. 'Because I'm not allowing this town to organise another damn vigilante group.' As they had fifteen years ago.

When Blake had been fifteen years old, he'd been beaten up by a group of older teenagers venting their anger, against Blake's parents, on their own parents' behalf—a form of reprisal. It had been brutal and appalling.

And she *wasn't* letting it happen again.

She tipped the now cold contents of her cup onto the roots of the jacaranda. 'I don't want to receive a visit from the police with their lights flashing to inform me you've been taken to hospital. I've no desire to see you looking so swollen and bruised I can barely recognise you.'

She gripped the handle of the teacup tight. 'And I've zero interest in your damn pride, so suck it up, sunshine. If telling the truth prevents that from happening again, I'll tell the truth to the next hundred people I see.'

'You cried.'

She shook herself. 'What?' *When?*

'When you saw me at the hospital. When we were fifteen. Would you cry if it happened again now?'

She clenched her hands so hard she shook. Was he trying to make light of this? Or was he deliberately trying to get a rise out of her? 'Absolutely. But this time it'd be in gratitude that Iris wasn't here to see it. Make no mistake, Blake, I'm not doing this to defend you. I'm—'

'Doing it for Gran, I know.'

Something in his eyes lightened, though, and it infuriated her even more. She pointed at him. 'Damn straight. Don't forget it.' Before flouncing off.

CHAPTER TWO

THE FOLLOWING MORNING, also at ten, Nina found herself once again sitting beside Blake. And once again wishing they still had the kind of friendship where she could grab his hand so that neither one of them had to face this alone—the reading of Iris's will.

She'd never once in her life considered having to live without Blake's friendship. Oh, they mightn't have physically been in the same location in the last ten years, but that was just geography. He'd only ever felt like a phone call away.

Whenever they'd spoken on the phone, video-called or texted, the strength of their connection had remained. At least, that was what it had felt like, but in February when he hadn't shown up for her mother's funeral she'd realised how mistaken she'd been. And she missed that connection, their friendship. She missed it so much it left her feeling wrung out.

With her mum and Iris gone, and Blake clearly having left her behind years ago, she felt cast adrift in a way she'd never experienced before. She had absolutely no idea what the future held. How did she move forward from here?

You'll work it out. You don't have to sort out your entire future today.

Shuffling papers on his desk, Leonard glanced first at her and then at Blake. 'Shall we get started?'

'Whenever you're ready,' she said, not looking at Blake, not checking with him first to make sure he too was ready. What was the point? He couldn't be relied on and she had no intention of looking to him for guidance or direction.

But—

And if he didn't want her speaking on his behalf then he had a tongue in his head and he could use it. She felt the weight of his stare, but refused to turn her head and meet it. Once this was done and he'd signed whatever needed signing, he'd leave and she'd never have to clap eyes on him again.

She hitched up her chin. *Good.*

'Blake?' Leonard asked.

Blake turned back to the front, and nodded. 'Thanks, Leonard, ready whenever you are.'

Leonard Walker was in his mid-seventies and still fighting fit. Nevertheless, Nina hoped the people in his life were looking after him, spending all the time they could with him. Cherishing him.

Leonard opened the file in front of him. 'The last will and testament of Iris Catherine Day.'

The will was short and to the point and Nina

listened with a growing sense of horror. 'Hold on, wait.' She shook herself. 'There has to be some mistake. I—' Iris couldn't have left Nina everything—her house, its contents, her life savings.

Leonard surveyed her over the top of his reading glasses. 'No mistake, Nina.' Beside her Blake sat so still she wanted to push him off his chair just to get a reaction from him.

Leonard set his glasses on the desk. 'Surely this can't come as a shock to you?'

Her mouth worked, but no sound came out.

'The way you've looked after Iris these last few years…'

'I did that because I *loved* her! Because she'd helped to look after me when I was a little girl, and…we'd come full circle. It was a privilege to look after her. I didn't do it for *all her worldly possessions*. I knew she was going to leave me something. She told me so. But I thought she meant her emerald ring!' She'd lusted after that damn ring since she was four years old.

Leonard pursed his lips and glanced at Blake. 'I don't think Blake begrudges you any of it, do you, Blake?'

Blake shook his head.

'As for Iris's closest friends, I suspect they already knew her wishes on the matter. They'll be glad you're the main beneficiary, Nina. The people who know you know you're not some money-grubbing manipulator who'd diddle an old woman out of her life savings.' Leonard slipped his glasses back on his nose. 'Why has this upset you?'

Because she'd been taken by surprise. Hadn't known. That Blake...

Damn it! Was the man a robot? She only just stopped herself from pushing him off his chair.

Mind you, these days it looked as if it'd take a bulldozer to shift him if he didn't want to be shifted. Did he lift weights or something? When on earth had he developed arm and shoulder muscles like that or—?

He turned his head and met her gaze, raised an eyebrow. She pulled her mind back to the subject at hand rather than the disturbing depth of his chest and the intriguing breadth of his shoulders. 'How do you feel about this?' she demanded.

'Surprised,' he admitted.

She searched his face, but couldn't find a trace of bitterness there.

'She left me what mattered, what I wanted— Pop's watch and her wedding and engagement rings.'

'But—'

'I'm glad she's left her estate to you, Nina. You deserve it. I didn't know until Florence and Enid took me aside yesterday and told me precisely how much you were doing for Gran. You went above and beyond. I know you don't want my gratitude, but you have it in spades.'

'I was her official carer. I was receiving a carer's pension to look after her!'

'A pittance,' both men said at the same time.

'The money from my grandmother's estate would have had zero impact on me, and Gran knew that. It does, however, have the potential to have a big impact on your life, Nina. You'll now have options and opportunities you didn't have before. Good things don't always happen to good people, we all know that, but in this instance it has. And I, for one, am glad of it.'

'Amen,' Leonard chimed in.

Hmm… Why did she feel as if this conversation would be all over town by sundown?

Though maybe that was a good thing. It'd further lessen the chances of a vigilante group forming to run Blake out of town.

Who needs a vigilante group when you're doing a good enough job on your own?

Oh, stop it.

They signed what needed signing.

'She also left you these.' Leonard handed Blake a slim envelope with his name on the front, and then handed one addressed to her along with an A4 envelope that bulged. Leonard gestured to the smaller of her envelopes. 'You're supposed to open that one first.'

Right. 'Do you know what these are?'

'A personal message for each of you, I expect.'

He pressed his hands together. 'And may I suggest that you don't read them here?'

Her lips twitched. 'You've another appointment coming up, huh?'

His eyes twinkled. 'And I'm hoping to hit the golf course by midday. But that was also a little instruction from Iris.' He ran a finger down the page in front of him. 'In an ideal world, I'd like the youngsters to open their letters at my kitchen table over a bottle of bubbly. It's not compulsory, of course, but the thought makes me happy.'

That sounded like Iris.

Two minutes later, she and Blake stood on the footpath outside Leonard's office. They'd made their way to the solicitor's separately this morning, and she wasn't walking home with him now either.

Why not?

She couldn't think of a single reason. At least not one that wasn't childish. And somewhere in the last half an hour much of her anger had drained away, leaving her with little appetite for snark. In being named Iris's main beneficiary, Nina felt as if she'd won something and that Blake had lost. And yet she wouldn't have felt that way if their positions had been reversed—if Blake had been the main beneficiary. It made little sense, but it was how she felt all the same.

All of it felt *wrong*.

'You okay?'

In the mid-morning sunlight—which was basically blindingly bright—the blue of Blake's eyes was shockingly potent.

'Nina?'

She shook herself. 'Still in shock—discombobulated.'

He let out a soft chuckle that had all the fine hairs on her arms lifting. 'That still your favourite word?'

'One of them.'

He held up his envelope. 'We going to do this?'

'Absolutely. Not now, though. This afternoon.' She needed some space. She needed a breather. She needed time to gather her wits, and get her head around this morning's revelation. Apparently she was now the proud owner of Iris's house and the five hundred thousand dollars she'd had in her bank account. It…

'What time?'

Her brows shot up. 'Why, you got other plans?'

One side of his mouth hooked up. Had it always done that? 'Is that outside the realms of possibility?'

'If we were in Melbourne or Sydney, I'd absolutely believe you had things to do and people to see but here in Callenbook…?' She shook her head.

'Goes to show what you know, then. I promised Gladys I'd pop around and fix her back gate, while Enid wants me to show her how to use the new power drill she's bought. But I can be back at whatever time suits you.'

Bless those women. They knew keeping him busy was the best thing they could do for him. And the fact she cared about that went to show how hard old habits died.

'And...' He shuffled his feet.

Shading her eyes against the glare, she glanced up. 'And?'

'Guess I'd just like to ready myself.' He held up the letter. 'Get in the right frame of mind. These will be the last words Gran ever speaks to me and...' He rolled his shoulders. 'I want to treat them with respect.'

Rummaging in her bag, Nina fumbled around for her sunglasses and shoved them on her nose, blinked hard and swallowed the lump in her throat. 'Six o'clock?'

He nodded.

'I'll bring the champagne.' It seemed the least she could do. 'Later, Blake,' she managed, moving away.

'Later, Nina,' he said, moving off in the opposite direction.

Nina pushed through Iris's back door promptly at six, and then stopped short when she saw Blake sitting at the table. Her cheeks started to burn. 'Sorry. I forgot to knock. Old habits.' *Oops.*

'Your house. You can come in whenever you want. I should probably be paying you rent.'

She *very* carefully set the stainless-steel wine

cooler with an apparently *very nice bottle of French champagne* on the table before she threw it at him. 'You suggest that again and I'll be organising my own vigilante group.' Ouch. She shouldn't even joke about that.

He didn't seem to mind, though, giving another of those maddening chuckles instead. 'Who would you enlist?'

She chafed the gooseflesh from her arms. 'The Deadly Sins.'

'The big guns, huh?' He collected two champagne flutes from the cupboard. 'And what would my punishment be?'

'Thursday night bingo and Saturday afternoon line dancing.'

'What?' He nearly dropped the glasses. 'Okay, you win. I'll never mention the rent thing again.'

Good. She gestured to the bottle. 'You want to do the honours?'

'Line dancing? *Seriously?*' He clearly wasn't ready to let the matter drop. 'You *hate* country music.'

'Loathe it to the depths of my cold, dark soul,' she agreed. 'But here's the thing—I've discovered that country music is actually bearable when one is line dancing...or boot scootin' as they call it.'

His jaw dropped. 'You don't?'

That was what her life had become. 'Someone needs to keep an eye on the Deadly Sins.'

He gaped at her.

She gestured to the champagne. 'Chop-chop.' It felt like old times, but she hardened her heart against its inevitable softening. She didn't want to remain consumed with anger and bitterness towards Blake, but she had no intention of trusting him again. They *weren't* friends, he'd proven that, and she'd save herself a lot of grief if she kept that knowledge at the forefront of her mind.

'This is a really nice drop, Nina.' He peeled the gold foil from the top.

'I know.' She feigned a sophistication totally alien to her, but it must've been convincing enough as Blake didn't burst into gales of laughter.

Holding the bottle securely in one hand, he started to twist the cork from the bottle and she couldn't help noticing the way the rope of muscle in his forearms flexed and clenched. Those arms looked rock-hard. He didn't get those from working at a computer all day.

The pop when the cork released made her jump. She shook herself. What on earth was she doing ogling Blake's arms? If she wanted to ogle fit male bodies she should go to the pub on Saturday night when the farmhands and stockmen from the nearby properties came into town to blow off some steam. Or walk past the Oval on Wednesday nights when the footy team practised. *Not* ogling weedy little Blake.

Not weedy any more. Besides, he'd started filling out when he was fourteen. It was a long time since he'd been weedy.

Then don't ogle your best friend.

Ex best friend. That reminder had a chill chasing down her spine.

He poured the champagne and handed her a glass. They stared at their letters—both sitting on the table—and Nina pulled in a breath. 'Right, this seems like a good time to have a toast.' She lifted her glass. 'To Iris Day, the best honorary grandmother…'

'And best actual grandmother,' Blake inserted when she glanced at him expectantly.

'And best friend and advisor that anyone could ever have had. Granny Day, you'll be greatly missed.'

'Gran, you'll never be forgotten.'

They touched glasses and sipped silently.

Nina sipped her fizz, and Blake couldn't tell if she enjoyed it or not. Somewhere in the last ten years she'd become opaque to him, this girl who he'd always been able to read like a book.

Nina had never been much of a drinker, claiming it interfered with her caring duties for her mum. And despite her nonchalance when he'd said what a nice drop this particular champagne happened to be, he knew it wasn't due to actual experience.

Because Artemisia Reynolds had been in the bottle shop buying sherry when Nina had been in there too and had overheard her asking Nari Cho, the sales assistant, for advice. Artemisia had rung Enid afterwards and Enid, in turn, had told him.

Welcome to Red Neck Falls, population two thousand eight hundred.

Enid had counselled—instructed...*ordered*— him to treat Nina with every consideration. Not that he'd needed such counsel. He had every intention of doing exactly that. Enid had also told him how lost Iris would've been without her during these last few months. She'd told him that Nina had been an absolute rock and an utter angel throughout the entirety of Iris's illness. She'd said they'd have all been lost without her.

Nina looks after everyone. It's time someone looked after Nina.

Like the way she'd looked after him yesterday, when she'd told that Robbie kid that Blake hadn't known his grandmother was ill.

She'd said she didn't want another vigilante group forming. He rubbed a hand over his face. They were all adults now, though. What had happened to him as a fifteen-year-old wouldn't happen again. It was ancient history.

Except... He hadn't been the only one traumatised by that long-ago event. He glanced across at Nina. She was still looking after him, even when, to all appearances, she loathed him.

Tell her why you didn't make it home for Johanna's funeral.

Now was his chance. She was a captive audience. She'd remain here in Gran's kitchen until the letters were read and at least one glass of champagne consumed.

What if she laughs in your face? What if she doesn't believe you?

His stomach churned. Nina would do neither of those things. But his heart still beat too hard against his ribs.

What if she says you should've made a bigger effort? What if she says you should've come home sooner?

Bracing his hands on the table, he bent at the waist and dragged air into cramped lungs.

'You okay?'

Nodding, he straightened. This wasn't the right time. This moment should be about Iris, not him. He gestured to their letters. 'We going to do this?'

Her gaze raked across his face. 'We are.' Pulling out a chair, she dropped into it and reached for her letter, gesturing for him to do the same.

They turned their letters over and over in their fingers, as if reluctant to move beyond this moment. He glanced over at her. 'On the count of three?'

She took a gulp of champagne and nodded. He counted out loud. When he reached three, her fingers trembled as much as his did as they slid beneath the envelope's flap.

He pulled out the letter his grandmother had left him. *My dearest Blake*...

The rest of the writing blurred for a moment and he couldn't see a damn thing.

'Oh.'

His head shot up at Nina's involuntary murmur. She'd pressed a hand to her chest as if trying to keep her heart in her chest.

'You okay?'

'She says she knows my inheriting her estate will have come as a shock, but that she knows I didn't look after her with a view of profiting from it. She says she knows how much I loved her.'

He leaned across the table. 'Nina, how could you have thought anything else for a single moment? Gran *loved* you. And she *knew* you.' He ached to reach across and take her hand, but suspected she wouldn't welcome it. 'She knew you so well, in fact, that she started her letter with that reassurance.'

Giving a shaky laugh, she swiped her fingers beneath her eyes, before gesturing that they should continue reading their letters. He did as she silently bid.

My dearest Blake, I expect you're surprised to find that I left my estate to Nina rather than divide it equally between the two of you as I always told you was my plan. The thing is, we both know that you don't need my money.

Your company is worth eight billion times what my estate is worth (I know—I looked it up). I left you what I knew you'd actually cherish—things of sentimental value that one cannot put a price on. And, love, if there's anything else you want, tell Nina and it'll be yours for the taking. So drop any thoughts you have right now that my not leaving you my estate is a form of punishment or an indication that I'm in any way disappointed in you. That couldn't be further from the truth. Erase all such thoughts from your mind immediately—that's an order. Also, it would be a great kindness if you'd read that out to Nina. I'd like her to know it too.

Blowing out a breath, he rested back in his seat. Across the table Nina stared at her letter. Her mouth opened and closed. She rubbed her fingers across her brow. And then she glanced across. The expression on her face caught at him. He wanted nothing more than to hug her. 'You look…discombobulated.'

'So do you.'

'She wants me to tell you something.' He read out the relevant paragraph of his grandmother's letter verbatim.

Sagging back in her chair, she nodded. 'I'm glad she felt that way. I'm glad I wasn't part of a punishment.'

An ache stretched through his chest. It was a punishment he probably deserved and part of Nina thought so too. That was why Gran had wanted him to share her words with her.

They returned to their letters.

You need to tell Nina why you didn't make it to Jo's funeral. That and your silence afterwards hurt her badly—very badly.

Those last two words were underlined.

She deserves to know the truth. Please do everything you can to mend your friendship. I don't need to tell you this, but Nina's friendship, her love, is worth both our fortunes combined.

He couldn't explain why, but his mouth went dry. The simple truth of those words perhaps? Or the craving clawing at his insides to win back Nina's friendship?

Chatting to Nina had always been the highlight of his day. He missed that—their easiness, their laughter, the fact that she knew him so well. He'd let her down. Badly. He hadn't meant to and he'd do anything to change it if he could, but *she* didn't know that. Gran was right. She deserved to know the truth.

Glancing across, he found her staring at her letter and shaking her head as if in a daze.

Now, though, wasn't the right time.

Blake, Nina looks after everyone, but nobody looks after her.

The words were a direct paraphrase of Enid's. He bet his grandmother had left the remaining Deadly Sins their own set of instructions to follow. He huffed out a silent laugh. Everyone should have friends like that. He and Nina had been friends like that. Once upon a time.

Now, love, don't take this the wrong way, but you're out of practice when it comes to looking after other people. But will you please do your best to look after Nina?

Of course he would! He'd win back her friendship—somehow. But was that what Gran meant by looking after her? Or was there more she wanted him to do?

Also, I should very much like you present when Nina scatters my ashes. I'll understand if you can't manage that, I know how busy you are, but I thought I'd ask it of you all the same. I'm so proud of you, Blake. You're more resilient than you know. You're honest, you're kind, and you're smart. You've achieved great things and you ought to be proud of yourself. Best of all, in my humble opinion, is that you have a good heart—one of the best—and it's time you stopped protecting it and lived your life to the full. Not everyone is like your mum and dad, and it's not necessary to live your life in direct opposition to theirs. You don't have to prove anything to anyone.

Heck, Gran, don't hold back.

I love you, Blake. You deserve the very best that life has to offer. If I could make a wish for you, it would be that your life be long, and that it be full and happy. You have certainly helped to make my life worth living.

It was simply signed, *from your very loving grandmother, Iris Day.*

He traced a finger over her signature, fighting the lump in his throat. What he wouldn't give to have one last hug with her, one last conversation, one last hour.

When he glanced up, he found Nina watching him. She moistened her lips as if nervous. 'Iris has requested I let you read this later. She's left me a more personal… I mean this one is…pragmatic-ish. Sort of.' She thrust it at him. 'Oh, read it for yourself!'

He took the letter and read it. After her initial reassurances, Gran wrote that she'd left a more personal letter for Nina in the bigger envelope, but that she hoped Nina would do her one final service.

There's one thing I always wished to do, but I kept putting it off and now it's too late. I've always wanted to cruise the French and Italian Rivieras. Sounds fanciful, doesn't it? I've read so much about those magical places, though, have watched so many documentaries, and hungered to see them for myself.

Why had she never told him she wanted to see those places? He'd taken her to London and Paris, Barcelona, Munich… Rome, on their annual holidays. He'd have taken her on a Mediterranean cruise in a heartbeat!

There's a lesson in that for all of us, don't you think? We shouldn't put off doing the things on our bucket list. Make a bucket list, Nina. Those are the things that make life worth living. Other than that I have no regrets. But dearest Nina, it would mean a lot to me if you would use some of the money I've left you and take that cruise on my behalf. I'd like you to scatter some of my ashes in Cannes (the chance of running into a movie star!), Nice, Monte Carlo (the casino!), Por-

tofino, and then on down to Positano (the Amalfi Coast is supposed to be one of the most beautiful sights in the world).

He sagged in his seat, but kept reading on.

If you don't wish to do it, I certainly won't hold you to it. And I do want most of my ashes scattered in the pretty grove behind the church where the jacaranda is. I've always loved it there. And if you'd prefer to scatter all my ashes there, that's fine too. My darling girl, I've already asked so much of you, but if anyone deserves a holiday, it's you. If you do go I want you to add one or two places to the itinerary just for yourself. There are so many exotic places in the world to explore— Sardinia, Calabria, Crete. The world is your oyster. It's time to go out and experience it for yourself.

He gripped the letter so hard his knuckles whitened. *Look after Nina… If anyone deserves a holiday…*

He glanced at Nina, now immersed in her more personal letter. She had other envelopes scattered around her. Letters with destinations written on the front. Gran's dream itinerary?

Pulling in a breath, he gave a silent nod. Gran had asked him to look after Nina, and he was certain this was in part what she meant. What was more, it'd provide him with the perfect opportunity to win back Nina's friendship.

Reaching the end of her letter, Nina grabbed a tissue from the box he'd had the foresight to place on the table, dried her eyes and blew her nose.

He handed back the letter and tapped a finger to his. 'Looks like we're going to the Mediterranean, then.'

She froze. 'You too?'

'Her request to me was a little more generic. She asked me to be present at the scattering of her ashes.'

Nina folded her arms. Her lack of enthusiasm stung. He pulled in a slow breath. 'As she says, you could scatter her ashes in that pretty grove behind the church, but I know you, Nina. I know you'll feel honour-bound to spend some of Gran's hard-earned savings doing this for her.'

She stared at her hands and a lump lodged in his throat. 'I wish she'd told me,' he croaked out. 'I'd have taken her on that cruise in a heartbeat.'

Was it his imagination or did something unbend inside her?

He leaned forward, tapping a finger to the table. 'Let me arrange everything. It's the least I can do in the circumstances. And then let's give my grandmother the last hurrah she always dreamed of, yes?'

After the briefest of hesitations, she nodded.

CHAPTER THREE

NINA STOOD ON the dock and stared at the yacht Blake indicated. 'Our *own* yacht?' He *couldn't* be serious.

He shrugged.

She stared at the sleek vessel in front of them and tried to shake her head clear. Ever since she'd boarded the plane in Melbourne, she'd felt as if she'd stepped through the looking glass. She'd bet the White Rabbit had never organised Alice a first-class plane ticket, though. Or a privately chartered yacht.

Luxury yacht, thank you.

Maybe Nina should've expected this. Blake was a billionaire, for God's sake. Maybe this was how he lived his life these days?

Except that wasn't how she saw him. Of course she knew how successful he was—when his graphic design app had taken the world by storm she'd celebrated with him via Zoom, toasting him with a glass of cider. Back when they were besties.

But she'd never actually envisaged him belonging to this world.

She'd never in a million years imagined those long legs of his striding onto a luxury yacht as if he owned it, and everyone around him showering him with the kind of deference reserved for royalty.

It was kind of hot.

Don't be shallow.

Jet lag. Discombobulated. She'd be back to normal once she'd had some sleep. She crossed her fingers and followed him onto the yacht.

It was September, two weeks since the reading of Iris's will and twelve days since she'd seen Blake. He'd remained in Callenbrook for only a further two days before setting off for Melbourne and then to London. She'd caught the train from Bendigo to Melbourne on the day of her flight.

Blake had met her in the arrivals hall at Marseille airport, looking impeccably fresh and crisp in a suit that probably came from Bond Street or Italy or wherever it was they made suits that fitted broad shoulders with the loving care that Blake's suit did.

Thank God he'd ditched the jacket in the warm September sunshine, though. *Oh, right, and you think that seriously white, seriously crisp business shirt is any better?* He'd rolled the sleeves up to reveal strong forearms and had loosened his tie and the top button of his shirt. It was the sort of ef-

fortless sexy that film stars pulled off—and made
grown women weep.

She didn't care if they were best friends or not.
She did *not* want to think of Blake in those terms.

Then stop staring at him.

Plastering on a smile, she instead shook the
hands of the crew as they were introduced—the
captain, first mate, chef, a steward, and a deckhand. Seriously? Five staff for two people? She
gaped at Blake. He shrugged.

She gawked at the yacht's impressive interior as
they were given the grand tour. The general sitting area was flooded with light from the row of
windows that ran its length. The sofas looked ridiculously comfortable. There was a separate dining area, an office-cum-library, and an impressive
kitchen. Then came the bedrooms—four in total.

'This is the best stateroom, which is yours, Ms
Hoffman.'

It was larger than her bedroom at home, ridiculously plush, with an enormous bed that looked
seriously inviting to her jet-lagged body. A large
picture window currently looked out over the dock,
but would provide her with glorious views when
they were sailing. Yep, just call her Alice—Alice
through the Looking Glass…in first class…on a
yacht.

She swung to Blake. 'This stateroom should be
yours.'

'When you see my room, you'll realise that I'm not slumming it.'

And as that proved true enough she submitted to the arrangements without another murmur.

The fly deck—she was learning a whole new vocabulary—was accessed via an internal staircase and had a jaw-dropping sky lounge and an undercover eating area for dining al fresco. *Dining* because rich people didn't do anything as mundane as eat, apparently. On the stern of the main deck was a Jacuzzi—because of course there was. And the deckhand gave them an inventory of all the available *toys*—a waterslide that would whoosh them straight into the sea, a blow-up floating dock… jet skis.

Blake shook his head. 'There won't be any need for those.'

Her head jerked around. Why on earth not?

'We're not those kinds of people.'

He might not be, but…

'It's not that kind of trip.'

Speak for yourself! She and Iris had very different thoughts on the matter. When Blake turned away, she caught the steward's and deckhand's eyes, hitched her chin at the *toys* and gave a thumbs up. They both grinned.

'Why don't you go freshen up?' Blake suggested. 'And then we can meet at the sky lounge and have lunch?'

Oh, God, did she smell? She surreptitiously sniffed her armpit.

You've been travelling for over twenty hours. Of course you smell.

How mortifying!

She showered in her en-suite bathroom with designer toiletries that made her feel like a queen. Towelling off, she tied the belt of the complimentary robe securely around her waist and went in search of her suitcase. Which was nowhere to be found, but upon opening the wardrobe she discovered her things had been unpacked. 'So this is how the other half lives.'

She donned a brand-new pair of white capris and a fluttery pink top in a silky fabric that had screamed holiday to her when she'd visited the online shop Iris had ordered her to use for holiday essentials. Turning to the full-length mirror and holding her arms out, she said, 'What do you think, Granny Day?'

In her personal letter to Nina, Iris had told her to do all the things she thought Iris would love to do, to have the holiday Iris herself would've loved.

My dear girl, you're in danger of becoming old before your time. Not your fault. Circumstances have worked against you. But you're not yet thirty and you need to push yourself out of your comfort zone and learn to live again, really live.

She'd memorised those words thrilled and in-
timidated by them in equal measure.

*I've enclosed several sealed envelopes with
the location printed on the front. Open that
particular envelope when you reach that port.
Inside will be a challenge—something I'd like
you to do. Something I wish I could be there
to do with you.*

Her eyes had filled with tears when she'd read
that. They filled again now. Iris continued to look
after her from beyond the grave. Reverently pulling
the pile of envelopes from her handbag, she placed
them in the top drawer of her bedside table. With
one last glance in the mirror, and a wistful glance
at the bed, she slipped her feet into a pair of sandals, grabbed her hat and sunnies, and headed up
to the sky lounge for lunch.

She was greeted with platters full of clever
things made with prawns and smoked salmon,
along with colourful salads and crusty artisan
bread. Her mouth watered in appreciation. Blake
had showered and changed too.

Though that had *nothing* to do with the way
her mouth watered. He now wore a pair of navy
cargo shorts that showed off long, tanned legs, and
a polo shirt that hinted at an intriguing whorl of
hair at his chest. Uh-huh, and the least said about
that, the better.

The view! She swung to take it in, her heart thumping out a funny offbeat rhythm. The sight of the city from the marina was spectacular.

'Champagne?' Aurelia, the steward, presented a bottle of something probably amazing.

'Oh, um…orange juice for me, thank you.'

'You could always have a mimosa—half and half?'

Aurelia was Venezuelan and had eyes that twinkled devilishly. Iris would've loved her. 'Oh, go on, then.' She was on holiday after all.

Blake raised an eyebrow. She raised hers back as she took a seat. 'Problem?'

'It's not like you to drink on an empty stomach.'

'It's not going to be empty long. I'm starving.' She piled food onto her plate. 'I would also advance the theory, Blake, that these days you don't actually know me at all.'

His eyes went dark and broody. A part of her deeply resented having to share this trip with him, but it was what Iris wanted and she couldn't forget that. Blake might have failed spectacularly on the friend front, but Iris had loved him. Other than when they scattered Iris's ashes, they didn't need to spend much time in each other's company.

She ate. Everything was amazing. Blake barely touched a thing, though, and this was his actual time zone—his actual lunchtime rather than her actual bedtime.

But she was determined to get her body used to

the new time zone pronto. She'd read that plenty of sunlight and eating at the proper times would get her circadian rhythms on track. No matter how much she wanted to, she wasn't crawling into that tempting bed before nightfall.

'So, do the arrangements meet with your approval?'

She set her cutlery down. Was she expected to gush? Was that why he sat there so broody and silent, the picture of malcontent? She moistened suddenly dry lips. 'You do know I wasn't expecting a first-class flight or for you to hire us a privately chartered *luxury* yacht?'

'I know.'

'Good.' She nodded. 'It's lovely, all of it, thank you.' He'd gone to a lot of trouble. And expense. And she wasn't an ingrate, but if he was trying to get back into her good books with this show of wealth it wasn't going to work, and the sooner he knew that, the better. 'Why?' She gestured around. 'Why all of this?'

He sipped his sensible black coffee and she wondered if she was the only one in danger of growing old before her time. He was the one who'd decided to travel like this. Why wasn't he making the most of it?

His eyes suddenly narrowed. 'Why do *you* think I've done this?'

She peeled a prawn and ate it to hide the fact that her appetite had vanished. 'I think you feel guilty about not coming home for Mum's funeral, and I expect this is part of some elaborate attempt to allay your guilt and make you feel better.'

He was silent for a long moment. The sound of seagulls and jangling moorings filled the air. Eventually he gave a slow nod. 'Don't get me wrong, I'm gutted I didn't make it to Johanna's funeral...'

Don't snort. It's not elegant.

'Fact is, I based every single decision I made in relation to this trip on what I thought Gran would love and have most relished.'

The prawn churned in her stomach and she immediately regretted eating it. Damn and blast. Now she felt the size of a flea.

'I had no other agenda.'

Right. 'I'm sorry.' The words emerged stilted and wooden from a throat that had grown too tight.

He shrugged.

Not looking at the shoulders.

'As you pointed out, we barely know each other these days. But this—' he glanced around the deck '—is the trip I wished I'd had the chance to take with my grandmother.'

It occurred to her at that moment that he might not be any happier that she was here than she was about being here with him. The fact he hadn't appeared at her mother's funeral had already informed her of how little she actually meant to him. But the thought cut her to the quick again now.

'Look, Nina—'

'The captain would like you to know we'll be leaving for Cannes at four o'clock. We're berthing in the bay. Would you like to go ashore when we arrive?'

Blake shook his head. 'We'll eat on board this evening, thank you.'

She waited for the steward to disappear back inside before lifting her drink to her lips. 'Are you going to do that the entire trip, Blake—answer for me? I'm going to make it clear from the get-go that that's not on.'

He blinked. 'I thought… I mean, given all the travel you've done in the last twenty-four hours, I thought you'd like a chance to acclimatise and would welcome an early night.'

She stared back stony-faced. She had every intention of having an early night, but that wasn't the point.

He rose. 'I apologise. It won't happen again.'

He stalked off and she pulled a face, wrinkling her nose at his departing back.

Blake adjourned to the office *to do some work*. She contemplated the city, watched the bustle of the port—all of its to-ing and fro-ing. And then, when it was time, observed with fascination the manoeuvres that departure involved, before hitting the Jacuzzi. *You'd have loved this, Iris.*

She raised her champagne flute of mimosa at the sky. If Blake weren't on board it'd be just about perfect.

The first thing Nina did when she woke the next morning—early—was seize the envelope marked Cannes.

Your challenge today is to find an exclusive boutique and buy a bikini, Nina. And I want you to splash out a ridiculous amount of money on it too. Penny-pinching is sometimes necessary, but not on this trip. You deserve to splurge and spoil yourself. And then I want you to head down to the beach with a sunhat and a pair of sunnies, and stretch yourself out on one of those sun loungers under a big umbrella and soak up the atmosphere.

Her jaw dropped.
There were a couple of additional notes:

The bikini can't be some dull colour like black or navy, either. Make it something colourful, something happy, something a woman in a film would wear. And don't forget the sunscreen!

A bikini? She'd never worn a bikini in her life! They were so *little*. They covered nothing more than the bare essentials, and sometimes not even that.
Her in a bikini? She couldn't—
You're in danger of becoming old before your time.
Her chin came up. She was on a luxury yacht.

She was living the high life. Fake it till you make it. She could lie on a beach on the French Riviera wearing a bikini. She could be the picture of aloof sophistication. A grin stretched across her face. 'Challenge accepted.'

Opening his eyes, Blake rested his hands behind his head and stared at the bright morning light that played across the walls of his cabin and listened to the sound of water splashing against the hull. He'd slept later than he'd meant to, but after tossing and turning all night he'd fallen asleep only as dawn had started to filter into his room. Water reflections now danced around his bed. It looked idyllic. It sounded idyllic. In reality, though, he was in hell.

Because yesterday he'd finally realised how much Nina loathed him.

She'd arrived in Marseille airport, bedraggled and tired, but her eyes had been alive with interest and excitement. She'd never travelled before—had never had the opportunity. He'd grinned, wanting to share in that excitement. And then her eyes had landed on him and their expression had dulled and flattened and her lips had pressed into a thin line, and it had left him gutted.

He'd been viewing this trip as an opportunity to break down her barriers, heal her hurt feelings, and make things right between them again. She, though, could barely tolerate the sight of him. It had left him smarting, and feeling worthless and small.

And curt and uncommunicative.

Not that she'd seemed to care about that. The less he said, the less she'd had to respond to him, and the better she'd seemed to like it. What an unholy mess. For a brief moment, he'd considered excusing himself, returning to London, and leaving her to the cruise in peace.

Running away again?

Or, trying to make her happy, he countered with a scowl.

A part of him wanted to roar at her for reading the worst into his actions—for thinking that his not turning up to Johanna's funeral meant he hadn't cared. She knew him better than that! She knew—

What exactly have you given her in the last decade?

The question burned through him. He'd taken all the support Nina had offered, but what had he given back?

For the last three years Nina had asked him to come home for Christmas. 'Just for a few days. I know how much you hate this place, but it would mean the world to your gran and my mum.'

When he'd left Callenbrook, he'd sworn to only ever return for emergencies. Christmas wasn't an emergency, and everything inside him had rebelled and resisted at returning. He knew that one day he'd have to—that circumstances would demand it of him. But like a child, he'd turned his face to the wall and refused to see the obvious—that the people he'd left behind had *not* remained preserved in time, they *hadn't* remained exactly the same as when he'd left them.

Instead of returning, he'd invited Nina to holiday with him instead, but she'd refused to leave her mum for the holidays, and there'd been no question of Auntie Jo joining them. Things had become increasingly difficult for her and he'd—

He rubbed a hand over his face. To his shame he hadn't returned while she'd been alive. They'd had their video chats. He'd sent her and his gran flowers every few weeks. And he'd continued to put off going home until he'd unconsciously inflated returning to nightmarish proportions. When he'd most wanted to return, he'd found himself unable to.

When that first panic attack had happened, he'd told himself he wouldn't burden Nina with his troubles while she was grieving her mum. And then, when she'd refused to take his calls, he'd told himself it would be easier when they were face to face. He'd delayed telling her in the same way he'd delayed returning to Callenbrook and now it too was starting to take on nightmarish proportions.

She deserves to know the truth.

Gran was right. Nina did deserve to know. And he wasn't going to give up her friendship without a fight—he'd remain on this cruise. Maybe in fighting for her friendship he'd be able to prove to her how much he still cared.

Tossing back the covers, he surged to his feet. No more delaying. Over breakfast he'd tell Nina the reason he hadn't attended her mother's funeral was because he'd been in a hospital in Singapore having a panic attack. And that, as he'd had no hope of making Auntie Jo's funeral by the time he'd been released, he'd jumped on the first plane back to London to seek the professional help the doctors had advised him to get. He'd tell her about seeing a therapist. And he'd tell her how sorry he was.

'Has Ms Hoffman breakfasted yet?' he asked when he emerged on deck.

'She had a light breakfast and then she had George take her ashore in the motorised inflatable,' the steward said.

She'd *what*?

George nodded. *'Sí.'*

George was Spanish and young. He'd be lucky to be twenty-two. And ridiculously good-looking. Blake's hands clenched. Was there was a lascivious curve to the younger man's lips at the mention of Nina's name?

'She was excited to go out and explore.'

Without him? His heart slumped to its knees.

It shouldn't surprise him. It shouldn't leave him feeling so *lost*.

But damn it all to hell! She'd never travelled before. What if she got into difficulties? What if she got into trouble? What if...?

'Breakfast, Mr Carlisle?'

They were anchored just off shore and Cannes glowed like a promise in the bright morning sunlight. 'No.' He gestured to George, asking him to take him on the inflatable boat to the nearby shore. 'Did Ms Hoffman mention what she planned to do today?' He deliberately used Nina's formal title, wanting to preserve the client-staff distinction. Blake didn't take risks, and the blurring of such lines could lead to trouble. He wasn't letting that kind of trouble happen on his watch.

'No, sir. She just requested that I pick her up at four o'clock.'

'And what time did she leave?'

'About an hour ago.'

She had an hour start on him? What on earth would she want to do in Cannes today? What would she want to see? Would she want to do a city tour or maybe a historic walking tour? Browse the shops? Find the markets? Walk the famous Boulevard de la Croisette?

Why the hell hadn't he had the foresight to ask her what she wanted to do over that ridiculously awkward dinner last night? It would've provided the perfect topic of conversation. Except he'd sensed her jet lag and hadn't wanted to add to her weariness by making her engage in small talk that she wasn't the least bit interested in. So he'd sat there all wounded and broody while she'd admired a stunning sunset and stifled her yawns.

Every single decision he'd made since seeing Nina again had been a bad one—the wrong one.

Not true. Taking her on this cruise was the right decision. The fact he was finding it so hard was his own fault.

'I'll ring if we decide to return earlier,' he told George, springing up onto the dock.

With a nod, George turned the motorised inflatable back towards the yacht.

Blake fingered the phone in his pocket. He could ring Nina... Except, she'd ignored all of his calls these last few months, and if she was still to ignore them now... He dragged a hand through his hair, his chest cramping and greyness darkening the edges of his vision. He concentrated on his breathing.

Once the tightness had eased he lifted his head. *Concentrate.* If he were Nina, where would he go?

He sifted through the options before turning his feet in the direction of the Boulevard de la Croisette—the world-famous promenade with its ocean views, mix of private and public beaches, and upscale shopping.

He'd been walking for over an hour, backtracking here and there, and had almost given up. He'd been scanning the public beaches for a glimpse of her, had stuck his head inside the boutiques he'd thought might've caught her eye. All the while lecturing himself about not pouncing on her when he saw her and berating her for leaving the yacht without telling him. He'd act cool, calm and they'd come to some adult arrangement about letting each other know where they were at all times. Just in case something happened.

His jaw dropped when he finally did spot her— in the last place he expected—on a sun lounger on a private beach, and she was surrounded by a group of people who were all laughing and flirting with each other.

He wanted to stalk across, seize her by the wrist and hustle her back to the yacht where she'd be safe from the predatory attentions of—

Can you hear yourself?

That mocking inner voice wasn't what stopped him. What stopped him was the radiance of Nina's smile, the sound of her laughter when it reached him.

Look how happy she is.

He dropped down onto one of the benches that lined the path, shaded by the palms and the pines that marched along the avenue. His heart thundered in his ears, an ache gathering beneath his breastbone. When was the last time he'd actually seen Nina smile and laugh like that?

Sure, they'd laughed together on their video calls, but over the last couple of years those calls had grown less frequent—the pressures of work, the different time zones, and, he now suspected, her mother's worsening condition had all conspired against them. Why hadn't he looked beneath Nina's cheerful facade? She'd seemed happy, so he'd automatically assumed all was well. But...

Nina had been caring for her mother for what felt like forever, but it had always had an inbuilt end date. One he'd refused to let himself think about. Nina, though, hadn't had that luxury. She'd basically watched her mother die. And then almost immediately had watched his grandmother die—two of the most important people in her life.

While he'd been wrestling with a teenage trauma that he should've dealt with years ago, she'd been dealing with hard reality and cold facts. He dragged a hand down his face, recalling the attack that had happened fifteen years ago as if it were only yesterday. The conflagration of hostility that had erupted around him. And his realisation, once it had him cornered, that he was powerless to avoid it. There'd been no chance to try and reason his way out of it, no chance to run. All he'd been able to do was try and withstand the furious barrage of fists and feet that had rained down on him— the savage punches and brutal kicks he'd thought would break bones. He'd curled his body in on itself and covered his head with his hands and gritted his teeth, determined to not make a sound.

But even behind his eyelids the stony, merciless expression on Ralph Hutchinson's face had tormented him. At the time he'd thought he'd deserved all of it—all of the fury, all of the retribution. If he hadn't created the accounting package his mother had asked him to, she'd never have had the means to defraud anyone. Not that he'd known then that was what she'd planned to use it for.

He should've accepted the counselling he'd been offered after the attack had first happened. He should've sought counselling at university when nightmares had him waking in a lather of sweat. And afterwards too, once Drawing Board, his company, had taken off. Instead he'd kept burying it, telling himself it was all in the past.

He wished with all his might now that he'd sought that counselling. Maybe then, when Nina had needed him, he'd have been there for her. Instead he'd been nowhere to be found, and he couldn't blame her for losing faith in him.

For the last few years Nina had been surrounded with death. And now here she was on one of the most glamorous beaches in the world making friends with like-minded holidaymakers. The sun was shining, the air was warm, and the scent of salt and mimosa spiced the air. How, for a single moment, could he begrudge her any of that?

She deserved a chance to relax, to unwind, to remind herself of all the good things life still had to offer her.

His grandmother was right. He was out of practice at looking after other people. He liked being a lone wolf, a solitary entity—responsible for no

one but himself and with no one constantly looking over his shoulder asking him to justify himself. But Nina wasn't *other people* and for her he'd
make an effort and go the extra mile. Because it
struck him that when his grandmother had asked
him to look after Nina, *this* was what she'd meant.
To help Nina relax and laugh again, to help her
find joy in her life.

Nina, stretched out on her sun lounger, was par-
tially obscured by the two people sitting on the sun
lounger to this side of her. But then several mem-
bers of the group rose and made their way down
to the water's edge, Nina included. And then he
saw what she was wearing.

Or *wasn't* wearing.

His jaw dropped. She— It—

Her bikini, all shimmering gold with big bows
at the sides, was plastered against her magnificent
body leaving very little to the imagination. And
his imagination immediately went into overdrive,
supplying him with the missing details!

Heat gathered at his nape and collected in his
veins. Damn it all to hell. He ran a finger around
his collar. She had long legs that went on forever,
hips that swayed with an innate sensuality, and
the curves of her breasts were cupped so lovingly
by the material of her bikini top that red-hot need
pulsed through him in dizzying waves.

He couldn't start thinking about Nina like this!

He stood, wiped the perspiration from his brow. He'd leave her to have her fun and—

That was the moment he noticed the appreciative appraisals the other men sent her when she wasn't watching and promptly sank back down.

Folding his arms, he nodded. *Doing exactly what you asked of me, Gran. I'm looking after Nina.*

CHAPTER FOUR

NINA SLID HER sunglasses on her nose and planted her hat on her head. Both brand-new and utterly unnecessary—she'd brought her old from-home ones with her—but maybe that had been the point. Anyway, the sales assistant had convinced her that they'd gone perfectly with her bikini, that the outfit was incomplete without them, and she'd been happy to be convinced.

She'd sunned herself on a beach in the French Riviera in an eye-wateringly expensive bikini, had made friends with a group of light-hearted holidaymakers, and had swum in the Mediterranean Sea.

Seriously? Where's Nina and what have you done with her?

Could she have been any further removed from her old life if she'd tried? She felt lighter, younger and… Something else that she couldn't define just yet. Whatever it was, though, it was positive—A Good Thing. Maybe Iris was onto something with ticking off a bucket list?

Humming under her breath, she set off along the

seaside avenue, relishing the warm air and the dappled light beneath the palm and pine trees. Dragging in the scent of the sea and the faint hint of coconut oil—

Her thoughts and her feet slammed to a halt. Frowning, she backed up two steps to glance at the man sitting on the bench she'd just walked past. Lowering her glasses, she stared at *Blake* over their rims.

He sent her a rueful smile, a small wave. 'Hey, Nina.'

What was he doing? 'Have you been spying on me?'

'Of course not.' He shifted. 'I mean…not exactly.'

Her brows shot up. She pulled her sunglasses completely off her nose. 'So that's a yes, then.'

'I came looking for you because I was worried.'

Her brows, which had started to lower, lifted again.

'I mean, you've not been overseas before.'

'And…?' She gestured for him to continue. 'I have damsel tattooed across my forehead or something?'

He rubbed a hand through his hair. 'I didn't know how jet-lagged you were. And when you didn't leave a note or tell anyone where you were going or what you were doing—'

One hand went to her hip. 'I wasn't aware that

one of the conditions of this trip was to keep you informed of my every move.'

'It's not! But for safety reasons it'd be a good idea to let someone know what you're doing and when you expect to be back. It's not hard—I'm heading to the beach today, or the shops, or doing a historic walking tour, and I'll be back at four.'

'If you were worried why didn't you ring me?'

'As you haven't been taking my calls recently, I figured you wouldn't bother this time either.'

He had her there. Huffing out a breath, she lowered herself to the bench beside him and shoved her sunnies back on her nose. A part of her wanted to remain stiff and aloof—and sort of bitchy—but she was tired of that act. Maybe it was the effect of all that sun and laughter. It had been nice—glorious, actually—to feel something other than grief and anger; to just, for a little while, not be weighed down with sadness and care. In her heart, she knew that was what Iris wanted for her.

Could sadness become a habit? Was that the real reason Iris had urged her to take this trip? Already she could feel her perspective shifting—as if the physical distance she'd travelled had also given her some emotional distance to view all she'd been through this year.

She'd been so angry at Blake for letting her down. And for letting Johanna and Iris down too—the two women who had loved him unconditionally and had practically raised him. She'd wanted to punish him for that.

But it didn't take a rocket scientist—or an ex-best friend—to see that he was in a stew of guilt and regret. It might not be her job to make him feel better, but she no longer wanted to make things worse for him either.

She stared out at the water—a bright breezy blue, the sand a luminous gold—and let out a long breath. 'I'm sorry you lost your grandmother, Blake.'

The shoulder closest to her lifted. 'I'm sorry you lost your honorary grandmother too, Nina. And your mum.'

She didn't have to stay angry with him and that felt good. But it didn't mean they'd ever be friends again. She doubted that gulf could be breached. There were only so many miracles the sea, the sun, light-hearted laughter and a ludicrous bikini could perform.

'So here's the thing...'

His abruptness made her blink.

'I came looking for you, and when I eventually found you—clearly having fun—I was going to leave again. But then you and a few of your new friends decided to go swimming...' He scowled. 'And I saw the way a couple of those guys were looking at you and I...'

'You...?' She couldn't explain her fascination. He rolled his shoulders, that scowl darkening, and nor could she explain why it made her want to laugh.

'And I came over all...'

What?

'Like an overprotective father or something.'

Shaking her head, she reached into her tote—also brand-new as it too was apparently a necessary accessory to the bikini—and pulled out her water bottle. 'I don't have one of those.'

Her father had left when she was twelve and her mother, *his wife*, had been diagnosed with multiple sclerosis. He was a lot of things—unreliable, self-interested, greedy—but overprotective wasn't one of them.

'Yeah, me neither.'

Blake's father was even worse than hers—*no* backbone whatsoever. He'd always fallen in with whatever his wife had wanted. Even when those things had been criminal.

'So I've no idea who I was channelling.'

How long had he been sitting here? It had been a couple of hours since she'd been swimming. She handed him the water bottle. 'You sure you're not the one who's jet-lagged?'

'I don't know what I am.'

He drank half the bottle in one long pull. He went to hand it back, but she gestured for him to finish it. Getting him back to the public dock where George had dropped her off wouldn't be fun if he was dehydrated.

Pursing her lips, she studied him. Today she'd been on a beach having fun and feeling young and carefree for what felt like the first time in forever, and he'd been sitting here watching her and being all broody and tortured. 'When did you become so…*stuffy*, Blake?'

He stiffened. 'I'm not *stuffy*!'

He looked so outraged it was all she could do not to laugh. 'Maybe *stodgy* is a better word.' She gestured to him sitting on the bench and then gestured far more expansively at the view in front of them. 'Acting like my watchdog is definitely the actions of a stuffed shirt.'

His jaw tightened. 'A one-off.'

She gestured to where she'd been sitting on the beach. 'I was with a group of people on a beach with a lot of other people around. What issues do you think I'd have had?' She thrust out her chin. 'And what if I wanted to generate some male interest? Did you stop to think about that?'

He started as if she'd zapped him with a hundred volts.

'Do you honestly think I've never had to deal with unwanted male attention before? I'm not some damsel in need of rescuing, if that's what you think.'

'Of course I don't. I…'

He couldn't finish the sentence and she nodded. 'I think you're the one who's floundering here, Blake. You're the one who doesn't know what to do with himself. Do you even know how to have fun any more?' She shook her head. 'Stuffy. Stodgy. Uptight.'

'I'm *not* stuffy! *Or* stodgy. *Or* uptight.'

'Or a control freak?' she enquired sweetly.

He folded his arms. 'Seriously?'

'Just calling it like I see it. I mean to *live* on this holiday, Blake—*really* live. Not merely endure or exist. I'm embracing this holiday in the spirit Iris would've wanted, and I'm not going to let you prevent me from doing that.'

She didn't say it in a mean way. She wasn't even angry about it. She just wanted to get that straight between them to avoid future arguments. This was a once-in-a-lifetime trip and she planned to cherish it. Who knew if she'd ever get this opportunity again?

Blake glared at the horizon. She glanced at her watch. There was a couple of hours yet before she was due to meet George and she was starving. The group she'd met on the beach were staying at the hotel, and they'd arranged for lunch to be brought out to them, but Nina had eaten sparingly. First, because she hadn't been paying and her offer to pay had been waved away and, secondly, there was nowhere to hide a bloated belly in a bikini.

She opened her mouth to suggest they get something to eat, when the air deflated from Blake's lungs. 'I'm *not* stuffy.' But he said it as if he was trying to convince himself rather than her.

Did he really not know how to have fun any more?

He turned to meet her gaze. 'I was in a hospital in Singapore having a panic attack. That's why I didn't make it home for Auntie Jo's funeral.'

She froze. Then she went hot and clammy. 'You…? *What?*'

'A damn panic attack.' He dragged a hand through his hair. 'The plane landed in Singapore. I waited until everyone else in my section had disembarked, but when I went to reach for my hand luggage…'

She stared at him. She couldn't form a single coherent thought.

'My chest cramped, my head pounded, my heart was racing. I couldn't breathe. I thought I was having a heart attack.'

Her heart thumped in horrified commiseration.

'An ambulance was called and I was taken to hospital. *Not* a heart attack, thankfully. Merely a panic attack.'

Thoughts jumbled in her brain. 'I doubt there's any *merely* about it.' It must've been terrifying. It must've—

Nausea churned in her stomach. *That* was what returning to Callenbrook had done to him? *Trying* to return to Callenbrook, she amended. 'Blake, that's awful.' She too sagged against the bench.

'To say I found the news confronting is an understatement. And as I had no hope of making Johanna's funeral—because, of course, I'd left it to the last moment—and I couldn't conceivably see how I could be of use to anyone in Callenbrook...'

Not of use to anyone? Her eyes filled. Was that what he honestly thought?

'I returned to London on the first flight back I could get.'

And he hadn't thought to tell her any of this until now? They were supposed to be friends!

'In truth I couldn't face the thought of having a panic attack *in* Callenbrook. Of triggering more of the damn things once I'd arrived there.'

That she could understand. 'But you made it home for Iris's funeral.' Had he been fighting panic attacks the entire time he'd been home? And all that time she'd been so awful to him.

'I've been seeing someone—getting therapy.'

She let out a slow breath.

'Because I don't *ever* want it happening again.'

She pressed a hand to her brow. 'The panic attack...is it linked to the assault when you were fifteen?'

He gave a mirthless laugh. 'Apparently it's not *healthy* to bury those kinds of traumas. And in not returning to Callenbrook for so long—in actively resisting it—when I did finally try to return it had become invested with too much meaning. Which blew the lid off...everything.'

She wanted to swear and not stop. A week after Blake's parents had been arrested for investment fraud, Blake had been bailed up and brutally beaten as a misguided form of reprisal.

His parents had stolen over two million dollars' worth of local money—and she'd understood that a lot of people had lost a lot of money and were angry about it—but Blake hadn't been guilty of anything other than having awful parents. He'd even had to testify against them in court as they'd persuaded him to create an accounting package with 'special' features he hadn't thought to question until too late. His mother had lied to him and manipulated him, and his father had stood by and let it happen.

His attackers had pounced on him after football training one afternoon and had left him with a concussion, several broken ribs, a fractured cheekbone and multiple contusions. He'd not just been punched, but kicked...and then left unconscious.

An eyewitness had said there'd been five attackers, though conveniently they hadn't been able to identify a single one. All they'd admit was that the attackers were youths probably a couple of years older than Blake. Nor had Blake ever named his attackers, claiming he couldn't remember the attack. She'd never believed him.

Her stomach clenched when she recalled the sight that had greeted her when she and Iris had rushed up to the hospital—the bruised and battered face with the eyes so swollen they'd almost closed shut. She hadn't been able to prevent herself from bursting into tears.

She hugged her tote bag to her and wished she had another bottle of water inside it. Or something stronger like brandy. 'You know who your attackers were, don't you?'

He nodded.

'Who?'

He turned his head but she continued glaring at the beach in front of her. 'Nina, what good will it do, knowing that now? It was a long time ago and—'

She swung to him. 'Every single time I go out on a date, I find myself sitting there wondering if this guy could've been one of them. It's *awful*.'

He swore. 'You *really* need to get out of Callenbrook.'

'And you should've tried coming home sooner, *obviously*.'

He froze.

Clenching her eyes shut, she shook her head. 'I'm not blaming you for having a panic attack, Blake. But I wish to God I'd followed my instincts back then.'

He eyed her warily. 'Which were?'

The blue of his eyes throbbed with a peculiar intensity and the depth of his chest and the hard-muscled firmness of his thighs penetrated her consciousness and had things tightening in—

What the hell was wrong with her?

'Nina?'

She ran a hand through her hair then resettled the hat on her head. 'I understood why you hated Callenbrook so much, and I understood why you wanted to leave. And, honestly, you had to leave—you were a software genius. You needed to go out there and make something of yourself. And while it's true that some people tarred you with the same brush as your parents, not everyone did. Half the town, probably more, were appalled at what happened to you. It was as if you had blinkers on, though, and couldn't see that. Instead you wrote the entire town off.'

And in some ways it felt as if he'd written her off too. 'Because of that attack, you wouldn't or couldn't see that there was still good in the place.'

The only good in Callenbrook had been Gran, Nina and Auntie Jo.

He rolled his shoulders. Okay, and the Deadly Sins…and maybe a couple of guys from school. But that was about it.

'Do you remember the night before you left for university? You told me how happy you were to be leaving and said, "I'm never coming back."'

'And you said, "What if me or Mum or your gran need you?"'

'And you said that was the one exception.'

'I told you I'd always come back if I was needed.'

He squinted out at the sparkling sea. If he

jumped in the water right now, he'd sink to the bottom. 'I'm sorry I didn't keep my word. I—'

'You tried. Which is good to know.' She stared out at the water too, but then her gaze swung back, pinning him to the spot. 'That night I wanted to ask you to return for something specific—like my twenty-first birthday or your gran's seventy-fifth or...*something*. I wanted to extract a promise from you. At the time I told myself to stop being so silly and not to burden you with thoughts of returning when you were so happy. I told myself not to be so selfish. But now I wish I had. It might've given you a different mindset.'

None of this was her fault. *None of it.* 'Fact is, Nina—' he tried to smile '—I just got too caught up in my own head. If I'd understood the outcome of avoiding the place for so long, I'd have done things differently. It wasn't your fault. Or anyone else's. It was mine.'

She shook her head at that. 'Not yours either.' She adjusted the brim of her hat. 'Right, so tell me who your attackers were.'

He had to laugh at her persistence. After a brief moment of hesitation, he named them.

Pursing her lips, she nodded, not looking the least bit surprised. Knowing Nina as he did, she'd have given the matter a lot of thought over the years. She'd have made her own list of likely suspects. 'I'm pleased to report I've not kissed a single one of those guys. *Thank you, God.*'

He didn't know how she managed it, but her words made him laugh. 'We were all just kids back then. Kids do stupid things.'

'Those guys were two years older than you, Blake. They'd have known what they were doing was wrong.'

'Maybe so, but the posse had been organised and the attack overseen by Ralph Hutchinson.'

She froze. 'The football coach?' She turned towards him, moving sluggishly as if in wet cement. 'Our PE teacher? The guy everyone looked up to.' She pulled off her sunglasses to stare at him. '*That* Mr Hutchinson?'

The very one. That more than the actual beating was what had shaken him up. Actually, it had gutted him. Mr H had asked him to remain behind after practice. He'd thought the older man was going to offer him support for all he was going through—give him some words of wisdom man-to-man.

He couldn't have been more wrong. Or shocked. Or devastated. All of the boys on the team had looked up to the older man.

'I should've learned—given my parents' example—that just because someone is an adult, that doesn't mean you can depend on them.' But never in a million years would he have thought that his coach would stand by and watch him take a beating with such a cold look in his eyes.

'Oh, Blake.' Nina pressed a hand to her mouth.

He shrugged. 'At the time, I didn't think anyone would believe the truth if I told them.'

She looked as if she wanted to burst into tears all over again, just as she had all those years ago at the hospital. 'I would've believed you. So would Mum and your gran.'

They would've, but then they'd have gone into fight on his behalf. There'd have been an outcry, a furore. There'd been enough upheaval in his life already with his parents' arrest, his realisation of how much his mother had used him and the fact his father had allowed her to do it.

His father hadn't been a bad man. But he had been a weak one. Blake wished he'd known at fifteen what he knew now—that his father's weakness had allowed him to become an accessory to the crimes his mother had been committing. His mother had dazzled Blake, but his father had always helped him feel grounded. It was his father he'd gone to with his questions, once he'd started to feel uneasy about the things his mother had asked him to incorporate into the accounting software. It was his father who'd assured him that everything was legal and above board.

He shouldn't have trusted him. He should've done his own research.

What then? a small voice asked of him. What would you have done? Would he have been able to withstand his mother's flattery and pleas or her demands and temper tantrums, her threats? Maybe he was his father's son, maybe he too had lacked the backbone to stand up to her.

He shook his head. He'd just wanted things to settle down. He'd known they'd never go back to being *normal*, so he'd contented himself with quiet instead. And in choosing that path, he'd buried what had happened and done his best to never think about it. He could see now it hadn't been the wisest course of action, but in his defence he'd only been fifteen.

'I didn't tell you this to upset you, Nina. I just wanted you to know that I did try to make it home for your mum's funeral. And I'm sorry I didn't manage it.'

She nodded, but she didn't meet his gaze. 'I'm glad you told me why you weren't there. And I'm sorry you went through all of that.'

He knew she meant it. But she didn't reach across and hug him as she would've once done, didn't even bump shoulders with him or reach over to squeeze his hand, and something uneasy shifted through him. His revelation hadn't had the desired effect and—

She surreptitiously stifled a yawn, and he squared his shoulders. *Give her a chance to process it all.* It was a lot and she was still jet-lagged. Plus she'd been through an awful year. What was that word she liked? *Discombobulated.* It probably described exactly how she felt.

He stood. 'You ready to head back to the yacht for a siesta?'

'Siesta? That's Spanish, isn't it? We're in France.'

'In French it's *sieste*. Believe me, an afternoon nap is universal in any language.'

That made her laugh and gave him hope that he could get their friendship back on track.

'Sounds perfect.'

Nina must've slept for four solid hours, but she turned up to dinner in the sky lounge looking fresh and oddly radiant. As if a day in the sun had been exactly what the doctor had ordered.

'What are your plans for tomorrow?' he asked as they picked up their cutlery and regarded their food with approval. Maybe he could talk her into—

'I'm meeting up again with the group from the beach.'

He waited for her to invite him along, and kept right on waiting. His heart became a dead weight in his chest. Was she still angry with him?

Hauling in a breath, he abruptly changed the topic. 'We need to talk about how and when we're going to scatter Gran's ashes.'

She cut into her fish and moaned in appreciation as she ate it, but then waved her fork through the air. 'I've been thinking about this and here's what I think we should do. We should go out and enjoy each of the places Iris has itemised on her list, and then as we sail away we should scatter her ashes while telling her what we loved about the place, and why we think she'd have loved it too.

Except there was no *we*, was there?

When did you become so stuffy?

He *wasn't* stuffy.

You sure?

So maybe he was a bit conservative when it came to the way he dressed and the way he acted in public. He liked to fly under the radar—keep out of the papers, keep out of the spotlight. He didn't want pictures of himself drunk dancing at some party with a half-naked woman or getting into an altercation with someone and having it splashed across the front pages or making some news clip.

He was more than happy to be relegated to the ranks of boring businessmen. Not that he *was* a businessman in the true sense, which was why he made sure his company was run by a group of accountants and financiers who were above reproach. There'd be no financial irregularities on his watch, thank you very much. Not after what his parents had done. There'd be no whispers, suspicions or suggestions that he was cut from the same cloth.

All of those things were admirable though. Not stuffy. Or stodgy.

Nina thinks you're boring.

He scowled at his perfectly steamed new potatoes. Nina didn't just think him boring, she thought him the antithesis of fun. She thought him a killjoy—*a killer of joy.*

'Is something wrong with your fish?'

He shook himself. 'Nope.'

One perfectly shaped eyebrow lifted in scepticism. That had always been an unconscious mannerism. He doubted she even knew she was doing it.

Keep it light. Prove you're not a killjoy.

'I'm wondering why I can't manage to cook fish this well.'

Cooking? That's the most exciting thing you can come up with? Good God, the women are going to be beating a path to your door, aren't they?

Nina stared at him. 'You cook? *You?*'

'Sure.'

'You *hate* cooking.'

He held up his hands. 'Okay, sure, I resisted learning for as long as possible, but I love to eat. And when I went away to university I realised how much I'd been spoiled by Gran's cooking. And apparently I didn't just love eating, I loved eating *good* food. So I either had to settle for eating mediocre food or learn how to cook. I chose the latter.'

'Did not.'

'Gran sent me tips, and walked me through making a few meals.'

'She never said a word.'

'I swore her to secrecy.' He laughed. 'I knew once you'd caught wind of it, I'd never hear the end of it.'

She set her cutlery down. 'Can you do a lamb roast as well as she did?'

'*Nobody* could manage that. But you remember her chicken and chorizo traybake?'

'Vividly.'

He kissed his fingers. 'I have it down to perfection.'

She stared at him—at his mouth and the fingers he'd kissed—as if she'd never seen him before. Things inside him tightened and clenched. He did his best to ignore it. Tried to focus instead on the mini victory of actually getting her to engage with him.

She shook herself. 'If you ask him, Calvin might give you some tips.'

Calvin was the chef.

She went back to her fish. 'What do you think of my idea about scattering Iris's ashes?'

'I like it.' He'd need to come up with something better to tell his grandmother, though, than: *I sat on the bench and watched Nina have fun with other people.* He couldn't see that impressing his grandmother any more than it had Nina.

'Good, that's settled, then.'

'I missed your cooking too.' He returned to his food. 'I wanted Gran to send me your recipe for that vegetable lasagne you used to make.'

'I bet she didn't give it to you.'

'Nope, said it was super-secret. And because I was an idiot I never asked you for it either.'

'Total idiot,' she agreed, but there was no heat in her words. 'And I can't believe she never told me any of this.'

'I'm not. She was the keeper of all the secrets.'

Her lips twisted. 'I *had* no secrets.'

He pretended to choke on his iced water. 'Not true!'

That eyebrow rose again. 'If Iris was such a vault when it came to keeping secrets, how do you know if I had any or not?'

'Because you told me so yourself.' He spread his hands. 'I have two words for you, Nina—boot scooting.'

She rolled her eyes.

'Is that *seriously* an accomplishment you want shouted from the rooftops?'

She stuck her nose in the air. 'I'll have you know that line dancing requires more coordination than you give it credit for. Memorising the dance steps can be a challenge too. It's a good workout, excellent for creating new pathways in the brain, and that shouldn't be underestimated. That sort of thing is important as one gets older.'

It hit him then that *that* was what her life had become—looking after older people and doing older-people things. Did she ever get to do young-people things any more? No wonder today's adventure at the beach had left her with such a glow.

'Don't look at me like that.'

He shook himself. 'Like what?'

'Like you pity me.'

'I don't pity you.'

'I know a lot of people think that way.' She glared daggers. 'But they couldn't be more mistaken. It was a privilege to look after my mother—not a sacrifice. And it was a privilege to look after Iris. And for another thing—'

'I *don't* pity you, Nina,' he cut in over the top of her. 'I envy you. I'd give everything I own to spend another hour with my grandmother, let alone weeks or months. I wish she'd considered me dependable enough to trust me with the truth about her own health.'

She stared at him, moistened her lips. 'She knew about the panic attacks?'

He nodded.

She immediately deflated. 'It's not your fault, then, that she didn't tell you. She and my mum did that all the time. I guess I did too, to a lesser extent.'

'Did what?' He had no idea what she was talking about.

'Tried to shield you, protect you.'

'From what?'

It was her turn to shrug. 'All and any harsh realities and ugly truths they thought you'd rather not know.'

His mouth went dry. 'Like…?'

'Like how much they missed you when you went away. They were careful to make a big song and dance about how proud they were of you and your achievements, urged you to travel blah blah blah. When what they really wanted was for you to come home for a visit. They always told you what they thought you wanted to hear.'

Nausea churned in his stomach.

'I had to do Mum's make-up for her whenever the two of you had a video call because she didn't want to look pale and ill and worry you. For the last few months Iris always put on her cheerful no-nonsense voice when you rang, even though it left her exhausted.'

They'd…

'They never wanted to worry you.'

His heart gave an ugly, sluggish kick. 'But… why?' They'd never shielded Nina in the same fashion.

She stared at her plate, pushing a pea around with her knife. 'Because of what happened when you were fifteen.' A sigh shuddered out of her. 'It was their way of looking after you.'

And he could see now that he'd let them. Because it'd been easier to believe all was well. He'd been a blind fool.

But he was done with all of that. He'd find a way to change. He'd find a way to look after Nina, just as Gran had asked him to. And he'd find a way to prove to Nina that he wasn't a killjoy. Maybe then she'd start to like him again and want to hang out with him.

Her eyes narrowed. 'You okay?'

'Never better,' he growled.

She grimaced.

He wasn't above using her momentary concern to his advantage, though. 'You up for a game of gin rummy after?'

'I, uh…' Her shoulders sagged. 'Sure, why not?'

CHAPTER FIVE

As THEIR YACHT left Cannes, Nina sprinkled a tiny portion of Iris's ashes into the sea. The water gleamed with the soft tones of the early morning light, all pinks, blues and silvers, and unruffled by even the smallest of breezes. 'I did exactly what you'd have wanted me to, Granny Day. I stretched out on a glamorous beach wearing nothing but a bikini, and I sipped a cocktail with one of those little umbrellas in it too. Truth be told, it was a little too sweet for my taste, but holding it in my hand, for all the world like some starlet… I felt like the bee's knees.'

Beside her, Blake gave a soft laugh and his face lightened, those usually stern lines softening. It felt like an achievement. She frowned. She didn't want it to. Where Blake was concerned, she didn't want to feel anything.

She pulled her mind back. 'Cannes was every bit as glamorous and golden as you imagined it would be. You'd have loved it.'

She gestured to Blake that it was his turn.

He turned to the water. 'I'm sorry to report, Gran, that I had a slow start—it took me a day to get into the holiday swing of things. Hopefully I made up for that yesterday. I took a selfie on the red carpet at the conference centre where the Cannes Film Festival awards are held—*Le Palais des Festivals et des Congrès.*'

He pronounced it with perfect French intonation and Nina found herself fighting a swoon.

'You loved watching all the hype and fanfare of the festival. Imagine all of the feet that have gone before mine on that carpet. Anyway, I figured you'd get a kick out of it.'

Blake's lips curved and Nina stared. He'd gone to the main film-festival venue? Why hadn't she thought to do that? Iris would've loved it.

You were enjoying beachy bikini goodness—sun, sea and laughter...a bit of light-hearted flirting. Nothing to envy here.

'And then I took a horse ride with a small group up into the hills. The views from up there were out of this world, and the whole place smelled of mimosa. I doubt it would've been something you'd have chosen to do at eighty, though you'd have jumped at it when you were younger. My muscles certainly let me know about it this morning. I ached in places I didn't know I had. But you'd have loved hearing about it, and you'd have loved my photos.' He stared at the water and nodded.

'Nina is right. Cannes would've lived up to all of your expectations.'

He turned back to Nina and gave her a thumbs up.

'You went horse riding?'

It sounded like an accusation and she couldn't blame his brows for shooting up as they did. 'Yep.'

'But you didn't mention that over dinner last night.'

'You didn't ask. I figured you weren't interested.'

He said it matter-of-factly and that stung, though she didn't know why. 'Yes, I did!'

'You asked if I'd had a nice day. I said that I did. You didn't encourage me to elaborate.'

Because she hadn't wanted to hear that he'd sat on a bench and done nothing all day, or that he'd moped at a table at some café, or remained onboard the yacht and worked.

She'd felt guilty that she'd abandoned him. Felt guilty that she hadn't asked him to join her on the beach. But it wasn't her job to look after him, and she had no intention of falling into that role. She'd done enough 'caring' this year. It was time to look after herself for a while.

And, despite his confession of the previous day—and it *was* a relief to know there'd been a legitimate reason he'd not made her mother's funeral—it had only brought home to her how far apart they'd grown.

And now to find herself...*jealous*.

You were on a glamorous beach with glamorous people!

Oh, but horse riding!

'Just for future reference, horse riding is newsworthy.'

'Do you want to know something else that's newsworthy?' He folded those strong arms. 'Even though you now know why I didn't make Auntie Jo's funeral, you're still angry at me.'

'Am not.'

'Are too.'

She rolled her eyes, but before she could respond Aurelia came out to inform them that breakfast was ready.

They followed her indoors, and Nina stopped short to stare at the spread. 'Way too much food.'

Aurelia smiled. 'I promise none of it will go to waste. Is there anything else I can get you?'

'No, thank you. It looks fabulous.'

Nina piled her plate with freshly sliced melon and delicate pastries and poured herself a coffee. She was going to have to start doing some serious exercise if this was the way she meant to go on eating. Swimming for real rather than bobbing in the sea; or maybe she'd take a few long hikes. Or go horse riding.

When Aurelia left, Nina glanced across the table to find Blake's startling blue eyes had settled on her. 'I understand about you missing the funeral.

I'm sorry you've been dealing with panic attacks. *Not* angry.'

'And yet—' he gestured between them '—not friends again either, clearly.'

'Ah, but that's a different thing than me being mad at you.' She bit into a mini croissant, gloriously buttery and flaky…and as insubstantial as their friendship. 'But it's true, we're not friends again, not really.'

He paled and her chest cramped. She didn't want to hurt him, but it seemed pointless lying about it. She abandoned her croissant. 'Not enemies either.'

'Why the hell *aren't* we friends any more?'

She hid the way everything had started to ache behind a shrug. 'That's an existential question and I suspect you don't want an existential answer. Fact of the matter is we've spent next to no time with each other in the last decade. How is any friendship supposed to flourish under those conditions? We haven't experienced each other's lives alongside one another. I mean, I have this view in my mind of what your super-successful life looks like, but I doubt it's the reality. While you have me living the same life I was living ten years ago, when in fact nothing could be further from the truth. So the short answer is our friendship has dwindled due to the effects of time.'

'Garbage.'

She hitched up her chin. Fine. If he wanted the big guns, she'd bring out the big guns. 'And due to a lack of commitment from both of us during the last ten years. You refused to come home. I refused to leave my mum. Other things were more important than looking after our friendship.'

His eyes narrowed. 'Not buying it.'

Would he buy the cold hard truth, then? 'Earlier in the year I'd have held the exact same position you do now. You want to know the exact moment I realised we were no longer friends?'

'With every fibre of my being,' he bit out.

'Yesterday on that damn bench in Cannes, when you finally told me the truth.'

'That was supposed to help! To explain *why* I'd let you down. So you'd know I *had* tried to make it home.'

'And it did. But it also made me realise something else.'

'What?'

She sipped coffee to ease the tightness in her throat. 'You knew how much it meant to me for you to be at Mum's funeral, yes?'

He nodded, heavily, as if his head weighed a ton.

'You knew how hurt and let down I'd be when you didn't show up?'

He dragged a hand down his face.

'Yes?' she persisted.

'Yes.'

'And yet you left it seven whole months before telling me the truth? I get that you had a whole lot more on your mind the day it happened. I totally understand not hearing from you then. But you didn't ring me the next day or the one after...or any time during the following weeks.'

'I didn't want to worry you when you were griev-ing your mum!' He slashed a hand through the air. 'And I was ashamed and embarrassed and...'

And they came to the crux of the matter.

She maintained steady eye contact and refused to weaken, although it felt as if a part of her were dying inside. 'That's the thing, you see? Your shame and embarrassment meant more to you than my hurt feelings. I wasn't just *mildly disappointed*, Blake.' She'd been gutted. It had felt as if every-thing she'd thought true about the world had been a lie. 'If we were *real* friends, you'd have understood how deeply hurt I was and made sure I knew the truth asap. But your pride was more important—your pride and protecting your image of yourself.'

He sagged back, a stricken expression in his eyes, and she felt as if she'd kicked a puppy. 'Don't look like that!'

'Like what?'

'Like I just knifed you through the heart. And don't say that's exactly what it felt like either.'

'Wouldn't dream of it.' He straightened and topped up both of their coffees from the pot. 'A knife would've been kinder, I'm sure.'

She choked, but then rolled her eyes when she realised he was joking.

'I'm sorry, Nina. Truly sorry. When you stopped

taking my calls, I told myself I'd wait until I saw you.'

She'd stopped taking his calls when she'd thought his *work* had been more important to him than her mum! And her. She hadn't been able to bear it; hadn't been able to talk to him after that. She should've known, though, that it had been a lie.

'I figured when we were face to face I'd be able to make everything right again. I was wrong, though. Clearly.' He stared at her, an unreadable expression in his eyes. 'But I'm not perfect—I'm human—and if perfection is what you're looking for from your friends, then I'm never going to live up to that. Nobody will.'

She gaped at him. He was trying to turn this back on her?

'But you're one of the most important people in my life and I'm not prepared to give up on our friendship. Not yet. Even if you are.'

Rising, he rapped his knuckles on the table. 'I have every intention of doing whatever I can to win back your friendship, to prove to you that you can trust me again.'

Oh? And how did he plan to do that? She refused to ask the question, though.

He stared down at her with pursed lips. 'I get the impression that at this current moment in time, though, you'd rather it if I'd remove myself from your presence.'

Absolutely!

'If I'm wrong about that, though, I'm hitting the hot tub. Feel free to join me,' he tossed over his shoulder.

No doubt he was hoping it'd soothe those horse-riding muscles.

Seizing her croissant, she tore off a piece and shoved it in her mouth, chewed savagely. No way was she joining him in a hot tub.

Why not?

Because these days Blake had muscles and she found them disturbing. She didn't want to think about Blake in those terms. She didn't want to think about him at all, but...

He's not the bad guy you've made him out to be.

Perhaps not. But somewhere along the way she'd lost the ability to feel comfortable with him, to be natural, and that was indicative of the issues between them.

Not his fault.

That was Iris's voice in her head and it made her stiffen. Iris would want her to give Blake a chance.

She glared out of the window at the perfectly sapphire water and the gloriously azure sky and the glut of morning sunshine. 'I'm not making any promises,' she muttered. None of it changed the fact that he'd left her stewing for *seven whole months*. How much longer would it have been if Iris hadn't died? Maybe she'd stopped taking his calls, but he could've texted her an explanation or emailed it to her or shown up in Callenbrook as

soon as he was capable of travelling again. He'd
done none of that.

She lingered over breakfast because, despite
thinking she had no appetite, every morsel was
delicious. Did Blake eat like this all the time?

Knowing Blake, probably not. But he could if
he wanted to and that was the point. Blake the billionaire—it was a side of him she'd never really
considered.

Shrugging that off, she headed down to her
cabin. They'd be in Nice soon and she wanted to
see what challenge Iris had in store for her today.

Ten minutes later she pushed the slip of paper
back into its envelope. Oh, God. Holy *holy* crap!
Iris wanted her to go parasailing!

No way was she wearing her bikini for this!

Before she could chicken out, she seized her
phone and made a booking.

When the boat pulled into a berth at the marina
in Nice, Nina ventured from her cabin to stand on
the deck and survey the city. Blake moved to stand
beside her. 'It's a pretty place.'

Elegant buildings stretched along the waterfront,
the intense blue of the water a perfect foil for the
long strip of white beach that stretched in front of
them. She took in the tall palms, red-tiled roofs
and an abundance of pink bougainvillea and nodded. 'Really pretty.'

He frowned as if realising her mind wasn't actually on the view. 'Do you have plans?'

'Yep.' With a superhuman effort she neither winced nor grimaced. A lump had lodged in her throat, making further speech impossible, though, so she pulled out her phone and showed him.

He stared at her phone and then at her. 'I didn't think heights were your thing.'

They *really* weren't.

He studied her face and pursed his lips. 'Are you sure you want to do this?'

Nope. She made herself nod.

'Why?'

'Because one ought to face their fears before they get the better of them,' she said, quoting Iris directly.

She noted the way his head rocked back, the way he paled, and shook her head. 'That wasn't aimed at you. I'm just doing what Iris wants me to do—' *literally* '—and push myself out of my comfort zone.' And she couldn't get much more out of her comfort zone than parasailing.

'Okay.'

He sounded far from convinced and she reclaimed her phone and tapped on an image to make it bigger. Everything inside her clenched. 'You ever been tempted?'

'Not once in my whole entire life.' A funny expression flitted across his face. He took her phone again and studied the picture. 'But now I'm wondering why not? *That* has the potential to be fun.'

'Are you for real?' She gaped at him, having

expended her limited resources of feigned insouciance.

'The view would be something else.'

As she'd be keeping her eyes tightly clenched the entire time, she figured that was a moot point.

'Would you like…? I mean, would it be okay…?' He shuffled his feet. 'Can I…?'

'Spit it out, Blake.'

'Can I tag along?'

Nausea churned in her stomach. He wanted to *watch*?

'See?' He turned her phone to face her. 'Two people can go up together.'

The churning stopped. From somewhere, she found a measure of backbone. 'You think I'm too scared to do this myself?'

'Not for a moment.' It was clear she had every intention of doing this—of going up in a parachute while a speedboat whipped her across the bay, high above the rest of the world.

Parasailing? That *so* wasn't Nina's jam. She didn't even like going up a ladder.

One ought to face their fears before they get the better of them.

Was she doing this because of his panic attacks? An ache gripped his chest.

She continued to glare at him, and he shook his head again. 'I recognise that look in your eyes.

You've made a reservation. I know you're going to do this.'

Whether she'd enjoy it, though, was another matter.

'But what you said to me the other day keeps bothering me. When did I become so stuffy? Doing something like parasailing isn't stuffy. I never do things like that. I always choose the sensible option.'

They'd disembarked and had started walking in the direction of the adventure company who ran the parasailing tours, but Nina halted now. 'You don't think this is sensible?'

'Not in the slightest.' He started them walking again. 'I don't think it's foolish or foolhardy either, though. It's perfectly safe.'

'Of course it is.' Her hands twisted together. 'Totally, one-hundred-per-cent safe.'

'It's just one of those fun for fun's sake things.'

'Fun.' She grimaced. 'Yep.'

She so clearly didn't want to do this and yet was oddly determined to do it regardless, and he had to fight an urge to wrap an arm around her shoulders and pull her against his side.

It was too soon to hug her.

If he didn't succeed in winning back her friendship he might never have an opportunity to hug her again. *Ever.* The loss hit him squarely in the chest, making his step falter.

She rounded on him. 'You *do* think this is dangerous.'

He gathered his scattered wits. 'I don't! I swear. I just…' His nose curled. 'I don't want to be considered stuffy. I want to be more like you—doing adventurous things and pushing myself out of my comfort zone. You're doing exactly what Gran has asked of you. She'd be proud of you.'

She blinked.

'You know what she said to me in my letter?'

She shook her head, her eyes widening.

'She said that I didn't need to live my life in direct opposition to my parents.'

Her mouth dropped open and it made him far too aware of how luscious and kissable her lips were. The thought had him gulping and turning back to face the front. *Don't think about her in those terms, you jerk.*

'Everything I do, I make sure it's above board, make sure it can withstand any amount of scrutiny. I refuse to do anything to court the tiniest whiff of scandal. I refuse to do anything that could cause people to draw comparisons between me and my parents.'

She swore and made an unconscious movement—as if to take his arm and hug it to her. He wanted to weep when she stopped herself from doing so. 'Hell, Blake.'

His nose curled. 'No wonder you think me a boring sod with the personality of a dishrag.'

'I *didn't* say that.'

'Not in so many words, but you basically told me to get a life.'

'I wanted you to do something more constructive than watch *me* get a life.'

'And you were right.' He gestured towards the bay. 'Never in a million years would I'd have thought to do something like parasailing.'

They both halted to watch a person hanging from a parachute in the sky, the speedboat below leaving a foamy wake of white behind it. She bit her thumb as she watched their progress. He could see the second thoughts gathering in the shadows of her eyes.

'You don't have to do this. If you don't think you'll enjoy it—'

'Yes, I do.'

She set back off along the footpath. He kept easy pace beside her. He wanted to ask her why she had such a bee in her bonnet about it, but some instinct warned him not to.

He pointed back towards the parasailer. 'That sure as hell isn't stuffy. And I know you just said I shouldn't be watching you getting a life—and I'm not… I mean, not in some weird stalkerish kind of way.' He frowned. 'At least I hope not.'

She huffed out a laugh. 'Whatever it is you're trying to say, Blake, spit it out before you dig yourself in any deeper.'

Excellent idea. 'You're leading by example, is

what I'm trying to say. I'm trying to emulate you. You're giving me ideas for how to be less of a kill-joy.'

She rolled her eyes. 'I did *not* call you a killjoy.'

'Nope, I came up with that one all by myself.'

'Your therapist has been schooling you in the power of positive self-talk, then.'

He laughed. He couldn't help it. She was terrified yet still able to crack a joke. 'My therapist and I have agreed that I'm a work in progress.'

Which in turn made her laugh. The brief affinity gave him hope. Whether she wanted to admit it or not, they shared a connection. His stupid pride had nearly severed it, but a stubborn thread or two remained, and he was determined to build on them. And he'd start by making sure she didn't face this terrifying task alone.

She didn't hesitate when they reached the adventure tour's small office, but pushed through the door and proceeded to quote her booking number to the receptionist.

'Would it be possible for us to go up together?' he asked.

The reservation clerk checked the computer and nodded.

Blake swung to Nina. 'Your call. I really want to go up, but I'll understand if you want to do this on your own. I'll simply make my own booking and wait my turn.'

She gestured back behind them. 'You really want to do that?'

Not really, but… 'Absolutely. In service of Operation Unstuffiness.'

She rolled her eyes. 'Fine, we'll do it together, then.'

Was it his imagination, or had her shoulders unhitched a fraction?

A short while later, they sat in a speedboat as it took off from the dock. They were placed in their harnesses and slowly winched into the air. Nina clenched her eyes shut and gritted her teeth, her knuckles turning white where they gripped the ropes of her parachute. Her teeth chattered. 'I've changed my mind.'

Too late for that, Nina. Way too late. Instead of saying that, he reached out and took her hand. 'For Granny Day,' he said as the speedboat gathered speed below them.

Nina opened one eye a fraction, gave a muffled squeal, and clenched it shut again. Her hand gripped his so hard it almost cut off the circulation. His stomach lurched. They were up so high! But a moment later his stomach settled and he stared about in wonder.

Under her breath, Nina chanted, 'For Granny Day. For Granny Day.' It soon changed to, 'Oh, God, Blake, you've gone dead quiet. Say something. It's every bit as awful as I thought it'd be, isn't it? And—'

'It's amazing. It's so amazing I'm speechless. I didn't expect it to feel...so amazing.'

Her grip eased a fraction. 'You're liking this?'

'I'm loving it.' And he was more surprised by that than anything. Glancing across, he took in her gritted teeth and tightly clenched eyes and affection welled in his chest. He wanted to make this experience fabulous for her too. She deserved to enjoy it rather than just endure it. 'Open your eyes, Nina.'

She did, but immediately looked down. With a whimper, she slapped both hands across them. 'Awful. Awful. Awful.'

Reaching across, he turned her chin until she faced him. 'Open your eyes, Nina.'

She shook her head.

'Please?'

A sigh shuddered out of her, but she peeled one hand away and cracked her eyes open. The fear in them—the panic—caught at him. He held her chin steady and held her gaze. 'I thought it might feel like a roller-coaster ride, but it doesn't. Focus on how it feels. We're floating and it's unbelievably relaxing, and it's also surprisingly quiet up here. And...'

'And?' She moistened her lips.

He shrugged. 'Oddly peaceful.'

'I can get relaxing and peaceful on the beach.'

'In a bikini,' he added, because he knew the bikini bit was important, though he didn't know why.

She huffed out a laugh.

'Okay—' with his chin, he gestured to their left a fraction '—we're going to look in that direction—straight out, not down—and we're going to admire the pretty buildings of Nice and the beach looking like a film set. Ready?'

She gave the tiniest of nods. He slowly released her, immediately missing the softness of her skin against his fingertips. They tingled where they'd made contact with her. What would it be like to kiss her—up here above the world? He'd bet it'd be spectacular and—

What the hell?

Not going there. Pushing the thought from his mind, he focused instead on her reactions. Releasing a slow breath and staring where he'd indicated, she bit her lip and nodded. 'Okay. It *is* pretty.'

Pursing his lips, he frowned. *Really* pretty.

'Why are you frowning?'

He turned to find her staring at him. He gestured at the view. 'I have all of this practically on my doorstep. All of these amazing places. They're only a couple of hours away by plane. Why haven't I been seeing all that I can see and making time to have experiences like this?'

'You took Granny Day on some extraordinary holidays.'

That was true enough. But he'd never thought to treat himself to something like this. Not on his own. Not just for him.

'You've been working hard, consolidating your company.' She sent him a small, not entirely steady smile. 'Operation Rejigging Your Life should take care of that, though.'

He grinned. 'Your name for it is better than mine.'

'I know.'

'So...how's Operation Out of My Comfort Zone going over there?'

'Ooh, swimmingly.' She grimaced, darting a gaze downwards. 'Hopefully not literally. Not entirely at ease, but...' she gestured '...this *is* pretty amazing. Plus I thought it would feel jerky up here—a lot of falling down and going up again, which I hate. But it's nothing like that. It really does feel like we're floating.' She stared around as if utterly confounded. 'We're floating above the Mediterranean Sea along the French Riviera like we're...'

'The most extraordinary people we've ever met.'

'Exactly!'

Her laugh made him feel younger and more care-free—like a better version of himself. 'Wait until the Deadly Sins hear about this.'

'They'll be so jealous.'

He met her gaze, pulled in a breath. 'Right... Now, part of this experience, apparently, is being dipped in the water.'

Alarmed eyes swung back to his.

'I'm assured that we just float slowly down, get

a tiny dunking in the sea, and drift back upwards. You up for that?'

She bit her lip.

He grinned at her and then waved his hands in the air. 'Look at me! No hands!'

Her lips kinked upwards. She glanced around and then down. She squared her chin. 'Oh, go on, then—for Iris.'

He gave the signal he'd organised with the skipper, and it was all incredibly gentle, though they both laughed at the shock of cold water when they dipped into it. And then they were immediately lifting upwards again.

Nina wore a T-shirt and a sensible one-piece swimsuit rather than that enticing bikini. He told himself he wasn't disappointed.

'I can't believe I'm actually enjoying this. Blake, I—' She turned to meet his gaze…blinked and frowned. 'Do you know that your eyes are the exact same shade of blue as the sea?'

The next moment her head jerked back as if the words surprised her as much as they had him. A spark arced between them—something primal, *carnal*, that had no business messing with things between them. Heat gathered in his veins, and once more a vision of kissing her filled his mind.

Stop it! He wanted to fix their friendship. Not wreck it.

He made his voice deliberately light. 'Was that a compliment?'

His teasing tone snapped her out of her trance. She stuck her nose in the air. 'Just a simple statement of fact.'

He wished with all his might that the skipper of the boat below would dunk them again. He was in serious need of cooling off.

Over a lunch of fresh oysters followed by steamed mussels in white wine, on the terrace of a luxury hotel with an extraordinary view of the bay, Nina sipped her wine. 'Thank you for what you did today, Blake. I did my best to hide it, but you knew I was petrified, and I know that's why you came with me, even though you weren't all that enthused about parasailing.'

'If I hadn't gone up I'd have missed one of the most amazing experiences of my life.'

'If you hadn't come up with me, I would've too.'

He shook his head at that. 'You'd have been fine—'

'I'd have spent the entire time with my hands over my eyes and trying not to cry. Instead, you helped me relax and see how amazing it all was. It was kind of you—very kind. And I'm grateful.'

'I admired the way you wanted to face your fear. And I meant it when I said I wanted to win back your friendship.'

She froze.

Damn it. She wasn't ready for this, was she? He shouldn't have pushed.

She eyed him for what felt like a very long time, as if weighing him up and assessing his seriousness. It made his pulse jump and jerk. Eventually she raised an eyebrow. 'So much so you'd spend Christmas in Callenbrook?'

CHAPTER SIX

NINA'S MOUTH DRIED. What on earth was she thinking? Blake come home for Christmas? She might as well ask for flying pigs! He might make a lot of noise about fixing their friendship, but in reality she doubted he'd want to put the work in.

Some of the magic of the day slipped away. It probably wasn't fair to ask it of him anyway. His fear of Callenbrook was a hundred times more potent than her fear of heights. He'd helped her relish their parasailing adventure in spite of her fear. But nothing she did would help reconcile him to the town he hated.

She braced herself for his refusal. It would no doubt be kindly couched. It pierced her to the marrow how much she wanted him to say yes, though.

Those intense blue eyes met hers. Her heart pounded in her throat. And then he smiled. It was so unexpected she sagged, her pulse racing like a mad thing.

'Christmas in Callenbrook this December?' He nodded, once. 'It's a date.'

Her jaw dropped. He'd do that? *For her?* She hauled it back into place, rubbed a hand across her heart, eyed him carefully. 'I mean, if you hate the idea...'

Shadows momentarily dimmed all of that brilliant blue. 'I think spending Christmas in Callenbrook this year—in honour of Auntie Jo and Gran—would be the perfect thing to do.'

Tears burned her eyes. 'They'd heartily approve.' *She* certainly did.

'And if it'll prove to you that I'm serious about fixing our friendship, prove to you how much you mean to me, Nina, then I'll gladly spend Christmas with you in Callenbrook. *Gladly,*' he repeated, stabbing a finger to the table as if afraid she might miss his sincerity.

She'd have to be blind to do that, though. It shone from his every pore, and she could feel it mending some of the fractures in her battered heart. She didn't know what to say and, as a lump lodged in her throat, speech became impossible anyway. *Don't burst into tears!*

She didn't want to reveal how much this meant to her. It was only early September. Christmas was months away. He had plenty of time to cry off yet. He might be making all the right noises, but it was too soon to trust him. As soon as he returned to London, he might forget about her again.

He eased back in his seat, framed by the gorgeous pastel stone of the hotel and a multitude of pink blossoms from a row of climbing roses that somehow only enhanced his masculinity. It had a pulse ticking to life deep inside her. His grin grew mischievous and she could've groaned because it made him look like sin personified.

No, no, this is Blake.

And he is seriously hot.

She squashed that thought flat.

'But can we please spend the Christmas after in London?'

The words shocked her back to herself. 'London?'

'Why not? I'd spring for your ticket. It could be your Christmas present.'

'Extravagant much?' She raised an eyebrow.

Firm lips pursed and she had to drag her gaze away. *Don't stare.*

'I'm starting to think that's something I need to rethink?'

She glanced back. 'What? Being extravagant?'

His mouth twisted. 'The fact that I'm *never* extravagant.'

'Ahem, if I could see our yacht right now, I'd be pointing it out to you.'

'That's a one-off. For Gran.'

He scratched a hand through his hair—seriously thick hair that gleamed in the sun, and she couldn't help wondering if it'd be as soft as it looked.

'I have all of this money, but what am I doing

with it?' He rolled his shoulders. 'I should be using it in service of Operation Killing the Killjoy.'

She rolled her eyes. 'We really need to talk about the way you frame things. You could've called it Operation Finding the Joy, instead. Anyway, I like Operation Rejigging My Life better. It's not like you have to remake your entire life over—just rejig it a bit here and there. As for what you're doing with your money—' she folded her arms '—I bet you're giving plenty to charity. And according to Iris, you have a *very* nice penthouse apartment in London with views of the Thames.'

He winced. 'That *was* extravagant.'

'And you shouldn't be apologising for that or wincing about it.'

'See? I'm a lost cause, a total misery guts.'

She couldn't help but laugh.

'And just so you know… I *am* joking.'

Blue eyes shouldn't look so warm. 'I know.'

'Mostly.' He stared at her with those pursed lips again making things inside her tighten and tingle. 'You always could help me gain perspective.'

She sipped her drink and tried to quench what suddenly felt like an unquenchable thirst. 'Then tell me why you think being extravagant will help you become happier.'

One shoulder lifted. Dear God, *why* did they have to be so broad?

'It's not the extravagance that's the problem, but actively being *not* extravagant,' he started slowly.

'It's as if, in being frugal with money, I'm also being frugal with joy. And I know money and joy don't have to equate...'

She leaned towards him. 'Nor do they have to un-equate.' *Why* wasn't he enjoying all of his money? He'd worked so hard for it.

'While I'm generous when it comes to treating my friends and work colleagues, and nothing was ever too much expense when it came to Gran, when it comes to myself... I don't indulge.'

She set her drink down. 'Why *not*?'

'I'm going to sound like an idiot.'

'Ha! Like that's something new.' She fought to keep things light and was rewarded with the flash of his grin.

'In some ways the money feels like a burden. I'm careful that every cent is accounted for so that nobody can ever accuse me or my company of embezzling it or doing something nefarious with it.'

A lump lodged in her throat. She stared at her hands with burning eyes and blinked hard. She *would not cry*. What his parents had done had left a deep and permanent scar. It had left him equating money with guilt and trouble and blame. It was the height of unfairness.

'You're not your parents, Blake. You're honest and ethical and generous and charitable. You've worked hard and earned your success. You've every right to enjoy that success.'

And she wanted him to. She wanted him to have

every good thing that darn money could buy him. Most of all, though, she wanted to drag him out from under the weight of that old guilt. It was misplaced. And if he wasn't careful it could crush him.

Because, despite everything—that old guilt, her anger with him, the panic attacks—underneath it all Blake had a good heart, a beautiful heart. Which was why him spending Christmas in Callenbook meant so much to her. His spirit deserved a chance to soar free.

Things inside Blake clenched up tight. 'I let my mother use me, Nina.' He was the one who'd created that damn accounting package. The one that had allowed her to defraud innocent people of millions of dollars.

'You didn't know what she planned to use it for!'

He should've known though, should've twigged that the things his mother was asking of him were illegal, but he'd been fooled by her attention— grateful and gratified she'd finally noticed him, flattered she'd trust him with as important a task as creating software for her investment company. He could see now how cleverly she'd deflected his attention whenever he'd started to become suspicious and uneasy. And his father had always been there to soothe his concerns, to assure him all was well, and give him a clap on the back.

What a fool he'd been. He'd thought that if he did a good enough job the three of them—he, his mother and father—would become a proper family unit, instead of him being shunted off to his grandmother's all the time. Not that he hadn't loved his gran. He had. But she'd had her own life to lead.

His father had continually told him he was a man now and that they both had to do everything they could for his mother—that she was a special woman with amazing talents. He'd told Blake how proud he was of him.

He'd fallen for it all—the flattery, the compliments, the lies and manipulations. What a mug! He ought to have had 'gullible fool' tattooed on his forehead.

He rubbed a hand over his face, wishing he could rub those awful memories away. 'I helped defraud millions of dollars from people we knew.' Many who couldn't afford to take such a hit.

Reaching across, she grabbed his hand. 'You're no longer that same boy eager for his parents' approval. You had no idea what your mother was up to or what plans she had for that program. She manipulated you, Blake.'

He recalled the sense of betrayal when he'd found out the truth. The shock. The pain. For a time his entire world had turned black and grim. As if a part of him had died. He'd been left feeling *less*. Less of a person. Less loved. Less intelligent. So much *less*.

His hands clenched. He'd *never* let anyone make him feel that way again.

Nina's eyes flashed. 'The woman was a criminal—she cared for no one and nothing but herself. And even if you had the slightest suspicion that her motives were nefarious—you were fifteen! She was your mum! Your dad was insisting you help out. We were raised to respect and obey our parents, Blake. Unluckily for you, yours didn't deserve it.'

Nina's ferocity, her fierce certainty, helped to temper some of that old guilt, but it couldn't touch the shock of that old betrayal or the coldness that gripped him whenever he recalled what his parents had done.

She thrust out her chin and all but glared at him. 'Anyway, you made amends. You testified against both your parents in court. And you've made something amazing of yourself and your life. You ought to be proud of yourself. And you ought to be enjoying your success rather than letting it tie you up in knots.'

He blinked.

She folded her arms and glared. 'So how's that for some perspective?'

'I…' He blinked.

'Right.' She clapped her hands together. 'How can we be outrageously extravagant today?'

Resistance immediately rose through him. 'We can't be extravagant for extravagance's sake.'

'Why not?'

'I…' He floundered.

'I just had a fancy meal and a glass of wine, which was pretty extravagant.'

'Yeah, but—'

'We're cruising the French Riviera and that's definitely extravagant.'

'I already explained—'

'And I bought a ridiculously expensive bikini in Cannes although I definitely didn't need it.'

But she looked amazing in it. As far as he was concerned it was money well spent. Would she wear it again soon? He hoped so because—

Stop it!

He blinked back into the moment to find her gaze had settled on him, an expression in those amber eyes that he recognised.

He folded his arms. 'That look says trouble.'

She raised a suspiciously innocent eyebrow.

'You have thoughts on how I should be spending my money, I presume?'

'Naturally.'

She pointed a not entirely steady finger at him. He stared at that small hand and a funny wave of tenderness washed over him.

'What you need is something fun and silly that will haul you out of your comfort zone.'

He pointed to the parasailers out on the water. 'What was *that*?'

'That was outside *my* comfort zone, not yours.'

Damn it, what scheme did she have in mind? Still, if it made her stop seeing him as boring and stuffy… His pulse quickened. If he could prove to her that he was every bit as brave as she was at facing his fears… 'Okay, hit me with it.'

'We're heading to Monte Carlo next, right? What could be more extravagant and crazier fun then hitting the casino? I'm channelling a James Bond film here—minus the violence—with you as 007, and me as…'

She was giving him the gift of 007? Could he pull off sophisticated and debonair? Damn it, he'd give it a red-hot go. Cocking his head to one side, he surveyed her—hopefully the picture of debonair sophistication. 'While I'm seeing you as Julia Roberts in *Pretty Woman*.' It had been Auntie Jo's favourite movie. He and Nina had watched it with her hundreds of times.

Nina's jaw dropped. With a visible effort, she hauled it back into place. 'Why don't we play at being high rollers for just one night? It's the height of extravagant frivolous fun—and legal,' she added when he opened his mouth.

He closed it again. Extravagant frivolous fun. James Bond. *Pretty Woman*. Maybe she had a point.

'You deserve to let your hair down once in a blue moon, Blake.'

She certainly deserved to.

'And here's something else… I know that as soon as you were able, you compensated every-one affected by your parents' scam.'

What the hell? Everything started to ache again.

'You didn't have to do that. What happened wasn't your fault. But it was a good thing to do. You don't have to feel guilty now about how you spend your money. It's been honestly earned.'

Some of the aching eased. 'That—' he stabbed a finger to the table '—was supposed to be a secret.'

She raised a pitying eyebrow.

He shook his head. 'That infernal town.'

His outrage slowly drained away, though, at the realisation that Nina's face was no longer shuttered against him. She'd fully engaged with him. Like a friend. Like a *best* friend. He had to fight an urge to drop to the paving stones and kiss the ground at her feet.

But then he couldn't stop from imagining taking one of those surprisingly dainty feet in his hands and pressing a kiss to the soft skin of her ankle and then working his way up her calf to the softer skin of her inner thigh just above her knee where—

He blinked, fighting an urge to seize the jug of iced water and pouring it over his head.

Nina, thank God, hadn't noticed. She stared out at the horizon, a brooding expression in the burnt caramel of her eyes, her pursed lips heavy with…

His stomach churned. *Grief?* Grief for *him*. For what had happened to him fifteen years ago.

Mixing with all the fresh grief she'd experienced in the last year too, no doubt. His heart clenched. So did his hands. Why hadn't he realised she'd needed him? Not just this year after her mum had died, but before that. How could he call himself a friend and not have been there to…make her laugh, make sure she had some fun? He swallowed. *To help.* He should've been there to help her through all of it. Some friend!

What had she had instead? Hanging out with old people, bingo, and *line dancing*. She was right. They could do better than that.

'If we're going to do this, Nina, we're doing it right.'

She swung back. 'What do you mean?'

'We need to look the part.'

She laughed when she realised what he meant. 'You don't need to buy me a designer dress.'

'Ah, but I *want* to.' Nina had never been interested in his money and she wasn't now either. He knew that. 'A designer dress for you and a tuxedo for me.'

'Oh, but—'

'A bit of extravagance is *exactly* what the doctor's ordered.'

She pursed her lips, before rising to her feet and tossing her gleaming river of hair over her shoulder. 'My dress has to be glamorous.'

He rubbed his hands together. 'Absolutely.'

Two nights later they strode into Monte Carlo's iconic casino. It was all royal blue and gold gilt and better than a movie set. The chandeliers glittered, the women's jewels sparkled, as did the crystal champagne flutes and whiskey tumblers that were lifted to smiling lips.

Nina's hand tightened at the crook of his elbow. She wore a stunning dress in red silk that fitted her curves in a way that made his mouth dry and his pulse stumble. 'Don't forget...' She leaned in close, smelling of an intoxicating mix of amber and jasmine. 'It's Bond, James Bond.'

He lifted his chin. *Debonair sophistication.* But his lips kinked up as he glanced down at her. 'It was so good, I almost peed my pants,' he quoted, making her snort-laugh.

'Stop it. You're ruining the impression we're making.'

'Ah, what you need to understand, Nina, is that, in an establishment such as this one, it's not manners that count but money.' He led her further into the room. 'We had to show our passports before entering, and there'll be facial-recognition cameras in the room. As soon as it's confirmed I'm *that* Blake Carlisle, we'll—'

A casino host made a beeline for them.

'Well, you'll see for yourself soon enough. If you want to appear sophisticated, don't blink an eye.'

It was all he managed to get out before he was greeted by name and offered champagne.

He took a glass from the proffered tray and

handed it to Nina. Her eyes danced and mischief shuffled through him. 'I'll have a martini, thank you.'

'Very good, sir.' The host snapped his fingers and a nearby server rushed to fill the order. 'What can we tempt you to this evening, sir?' He rattled off a list of games.

Blake glanced at Nina, raised an eyebrow. 'Blackjack,' she answered promptly.

They were led to a table, the bottle of French champagne left in an ice bucket beside them.

Nina threw herself into the spirit of the evening with gusto. Her enthusiasm contagious. The two of them had always played cards. Both Gran and Auntie Jo had played gin rummy and canasta. When he was at university, he'd played a lot of poker. All of that, though, had been for fun—not money.

The stakes added an undeniable edge of excitement, as did the glittering surrounds. Nina nudged him when a famous Hollywood actor strode past to sit at the neighbouring table. He nudged her when he saw a not so minor European royal and their entourage escorted across the room.

'Pinch me,' she murmured.

For a moment he saw it all through her eyes. She was right. It was extraordinary. Why had he denied himself this?

From blackjack, which amazingly enough they won at—they moved to the crap table, where they bombed.

'What would you like to try next?'

She bit her lip. 'Roulette?'

'The English roulette wheel or French roulette?'

Her eyes widened. 'What's French roulette?'

Grinning, he led her to one of the large bass tables and explained the game to her. French roulette was the big-ticket extravaganza that one expected from a casino. He laid a bunch of money on the table and a croupier handed him a big pile of chips that Blake pushed in Nina's direction.

She promptly placed the lot on the number twenty-two. She was born on the seventeenth of November while he was born on the fifth of February. Seventeen plus five equalled twenty-two. She'd always said it was her lucky number.

She won. She won an extraordinary amount of money. She stared, her jaw ajar. He grinned. From her other side the Hollywood actor congratulated her.

'I...' She blinked and shook her head. 'Beginner's luck.'

The actor handed her a pile of chips. 'Perhaps you'll be kind enough to do the same for me, then?'

She handed them straight back. 'No way. You only get one shot at beginner's luck.'

The actor grinned. 'No, you don't, you get three shots.'

Biting her lip, she glanced from the actor to the table. 'You can split your chips, right?'

'You can indeed.'

'Then put some on five and some on seventeen.'

He did and, to much applause, he won too.

Before they knew it, they were at a table with the actor and other Hollywood people drinking champagne and eating caviar.

When Blake and Nina finally left to return to the yacht hours later, Nina stared up at the sky and shook her head. 'No one back home will ever believe this.'

'The press photographer at the casino grabbed some snaps. I asked him to send me a few.'

She grabbed his arm and gave a silent scream. 'We ate caviar!'

Her excitement touched him. He wished she'd kept hold of his arm though. Instead she released it immediately. 'Did you like it?'

'Yes, damn it. Talk about champagne tastes on a beer budget.'

He'd order caviar for Christmas in Callenbrook. That had a rather pleasing ring to it.

The thought didn't have his heart dropping to the soles of his feet either. He'd do anything to win back Nina's friendship. Christmas in Callenbrook would be a small price to pay.

Seizing his arm again, she pulled him to a halt and searched his face. 'Did you have fun too?'

'Of course I did.' He'd been with her, hadn't he? 'You told me it would be an insane amount of fun, and you were right.' It was Nina, though, who'd made it fun.

A breath whooshed out of her. 'Good. I didn't want to be the only one.'

'Our entire table had a ball.'

'It's one of those nights I'll never forget.' She'd started walking again, gestured out in front of them at the harbour. 'I'm in Monte Carlo, I won at black-jack.'

'And bombed at craps.'

'And then totally cleaned up at French roulette.'

'Dined with a Hollywood star.'

'With my own personal James Bond. Who, it must be said, in his tuxedo, was the most dashing man in the room.'

Her words drew things inside him tight. 'Dashing, huh?' He'd meant the words to be teasing, but they emerged on a husky whisper.

She glanced up, her feet slowing once more, her smile dissolving, but the heat in her eyes remained. 'I shouldn't have said that, should I?' Biting her lip, she shrugged. 'But you really do rock a tux-edo, Blake.'

'And you rock a bikini.'

'And you shouldn't have said that.' She swallowed, but she didn't look away. 'You looked?'

'Hell, Nina, I can't seem to stop looking.'

Her mouth formed a perfect O, before she straightened and glanced around. 'And now here we are in Monte Carlo, walking beside the water beneath an almost full moon...'

Wind rushed in his ears and his heart thundered

in his chest. Every atom arched towards her. 'That sounded like an invitation.'

She raised an eyebrow. 'Maybe it was.'

CHAPTER SEVEN

NINA DIDN'T KNOW if she took a step closer or whether Blake did. What she did know was that she grabbed the lapels of his jacket and pulled him down until his mouth was in reach of hers and, leaning forward, placed her lips on his.

The kiss was whisper soft—like the balmy night air that brushed across her skin—and left her tingling, filling her with the same pale glow that lit the moon. As if this moment were from a fairy tale or a dream.

She eased away a fraction, their lips clinging until the very last moment, the glittering blue depths of his eyes blinking back into hers as if he too was caught up in the same dream. A line appeared between his eyes, not exactly a frown, as if the kiss had left him bamboozled and unbalanced. 'Nina?'

'Mmm?'

'You mind if we try that again?'

His words were a soft whisper in the night and it raised all the fine hairs on her arms and made her shiver with anticipation—*delicious* anticipation. She shook her head. She didn't mind. Not in the slightest.

Maybe it was the champagne, or the euphoria of the evening, or the romance of the setting with that big moon hanging above them making a silver path on the sea, the sound of water lapping on the shore. Or the sense that things had been smoothed between them, finally making all right with the world.

Cupping her face in his fingers, he danced those fingers along her jaw, sparking sensation wherever they touched, his mouth descending with an agonising slowness that had a moan gathering in the back of her throat. When his lips claimed hers, the magical dreamlike quality exploded, replaced with something far more elemental. An arm swept around her waist to hold her steady from the onslaught of sensations that pounded through her, before she found her balance once more and kissed him back with the same fervour, staking a claim of her own.

His quick intake of breath, his ragged breathing as they eased away once more—his arm still anchored at her waist, her hands crushing the lapels of his dinner jacket. She caught a myriad expressions in his eyes—shock, exhilaration, *hunger*.

Need, savage and hard, filled her every atom. 'Kiss me again.'

It was half plea, half demand, but he filled the

order with a flattering speed and they crashed back together. Her arms slid around his neck, her fingers plunging into the thick softness of his hair. One of his hands splayed against the small of her back, his other between her shoulder blades, pulling all of the things that most ached flush against him until the fire inside her threatened to become an inferno. She wanted to feel as much of that powerful male body against hers as she could.

And all the while, his mouth plundered hers with a wicked tempting sensuality, his tongue drawing hers into a dance until every part of her fired with red-hot need and an urgent craving for fulfilment. Arching against him, she moaned, she gasped… she begged.

He broke off to press hot burning kisses to her throat. Her hands explored the hard planes of his chest, frustrated at the clothing blocking access to the firm male flash beneath. Dancing fingers down to the waistband of his trousers, she started to tug his shirt free, greedy to explore the broad lean lines of him, but before she could, his hands on hers halted her movements.

'Public place,' he groaned out.

The gruff words blinked her back to reality. She eased away on unsteady legs.

His chest rose and fell. 'We should go back to the yacht.'

His eyes glittered in the darkness and she wanted to grab his hand and run—run at breakneck speed back to the yacht and see this thing flaring between them through to its natural conclusion.

Instead, she forced herself to take a deep breath. 'Not yet.' She backed up to sit on a nearby bench. She couldn't go back to the yacht until she'd worked out what she wanted to have happen once they reached it.

Closing her eyes, she fought for control. Two of the most important people in her life had died this year, and that meant she wasn't necessarily in a good place for making any kind of big decisions at the moment.

Blake lowered himself down beside her. 'You okay?'

'I think so.'

They stared out at the night, at the yachts bobbing on the water. It was a combination of navy and silver. The midnight blue of the sky and the inky darkness of the sea contrasted with the silvery light of the moon and the twinkling lights of the city. So pretty. So seductive. But it was a false promise, wasn't it?

The kiss between her and Blake didn't mean anything and it would never mean anything. She knew that. Because she knew Blake.

'What's going through your mind right now?'

She turned her head to find him surveying her. 'We're trying to fix our friendship and I'm not sure kissing each other is the right way to go about that.'

The fact she wanted to kiss him again—ached with it—didn't make thinking logically any easier.

He ruffled a hand through his hair. 'Damn, that flared out of control quick.'

He could say that again. 'Didn't see it coming,' she agreed.

But that was a lie, wasn't it? Ever since she'd clapped eyes on Blake again, a part of her had wanted him. Maybe it was due to her grief or her former anger with him…or the fact that she hadn't seen him in ten years. Whatever it was, it was foolhardy, and she had wit enough to know that.

'Way back when we were teenagers, you claimed you were never going to settle down. What was it you called yourself…?'

'A lone wolf.'

That was it.

Shadowed eyes met hers. 'I still am.'

Exactly. She watched the lights dance across the water like tiny flickering flames. 'I've no problem with sex for sex's sake, Blake. And I'm seriously tempted. That kiss was something else.'

'Yeah.' A frown stretched through his voice.

'And if I was never going to see you again after this trip, I wouldn't hesitate.'

He swung to her, the tendons in his neck standing out. 'But you are. You *will*. I'm spending Christmas in Callenbrook!'

The knuckles of his hands gleamed white in the moonlight, and her mouth went dry. They had too much to lose to give into this silly attraction. She let out a breath. 'That's the plan.'

He nodded. 'Good.'

'No matter how mature we want to be about the subject…' The burning needy tingles throbbing through her right now didn't feel particularly mature. They felt urgent and demanding and opposed to all common sense. Gritting her teeth, she did her best to ignore them. 'Sex complicates things. It's pointless pretending otherwise.'

Could she sleep with Blake and keep her heart from becoming involved? She'd had a taste of how badly he could hurt her as a friend. How much more could he hurt her—or have the potential to hurt her—as a lover? Besides, she wasn't convinced yet that he'd turn up for Christmas. To give even more of herself to him…

A chill chased down her spine.

'And you think our relationship is already complicated enough?'

He searched her face—wary, worried…tense.

'Things *are* being mended between us,' she said. They were. But if he let her down again…

'So why risk it? Is that what you're saying?'

His shoulders were oddly tense, so was his mouth. She realised it was caused by the same hunger that threaded through her in unrelenting spirals. *Oh dear God.* 'Yes.' She forced the word out.

They were both silent for several long moments.

'Your friendship is one of the most important

things in my life,' Blake finally said. 'I won't do anything that might risk it.'

His words should've left her feeling warm and toasty. As they rose to walk back to the yacht, though, she felt unaccountably grumpy. And frustrated!

They arrived in Portofino after lunch the following day.

Nina climbed up to the sky lounge, her heart in her throat after reading Iris's challenge. She still couldn't believe what she'd read. It was…

Don't think about it. You don't have to do it.

Of course she had to do it. But she didn't have to think about it right now. She wasn't doing it right now either, that was for certain.

Maybe later. Under the cover of darkness. When not a single soul was around. Could she put it off until they reached Positano? Or—

'It's something, isn't it?'

She glanced to where Blake stood at a railing and then in the direction he gestured to. Her eyes widened. *Okay…*

She moved across to stand beside him, but she wasn't entirely sure her feet touched the floor. Just…*wow.* 'I don't think I've ever seen anywhere more beautiful.'

Those broad shoulders lifted. 'Me either.'

They dropped anchor a little to the left in the small harbour. A dramatic headland arced off to their right, but in front of them the prettiest U-shaped shoreline edged with pastel-coloured buildings in varying shades of ochre, pink and yellow nestled between the clear blue water and lush green hill behind, dense with pines and palms and other trees and shrubs she couldn't identify.

She'd read that Portofino was a unique mix of forests—pine groves giving way to olive groves and everything in between. She hadn't expected it to look so harmonious, though. The scent of the man beside her—a heady mix of citrus and juniper berry—only enhanced the experience.

'You have any plans for the day?'

Skinny-dipping, apparently. Not that she had any intention of telling him that. 'Nope, you?'

'There's a monastery at an inlet over the hill that way. It's an hour-and-a-half hike through the forest. The views along the way are apparently spectacular. If you'd like to join me...' He shrugged. 'There'll be afternoon tea at the other end.'

'Sold!' She wanted to keep busy—needed to. A restless energy had kept her fidgeting all morning. She blamed the kiss of the night before. It had unleashed things inside her that were far harder to corral back under control than they ought to be.

Don't think about the kiss.

She was doing her best not to! But the effects of that kiss continued to burn through her. She ached with the need the kiss had created inside her. No kiss had ever done that to her before. She needed to do something to dispel it.

She shook out her arms. A hike would be perfect. It'd help her expend her excess energy, wear her out…and stop her imagining what it would've been like to have given into temptation.

Stop thinking about it!

She squared her shoulders. It'd hopefully stop her from brooding on Iris's challenge too. *Skinny-dipping?*

Oh, God, just thinking about it made her chest cramp. *Stop thinking about that too, then!*

Exactly! A hike with spectacular scenery? That would do nicely, thank you very much.

Thirty minutes later, she followed Blake to the hike's starting point. He studied the map he'd printed out, which left her free to study him. In khaki cargo shorts, his legs looked strong and powerful. Since he'd been on the yacht, his tan had deepened, and somehow that showed off his muscles to an even better advantage. What on earth did he do to keep so fit?

'Okay, this is definitely the right spot.'

She glanced up the steep incline and gulped. 'That looks nice and, um…challenging.'

'Up for it?'

She hitched up her chin. 'Absolutely.'

Blake led the way. The first quarter of the climb was a breeze, while the second quarter had her breathing hard. For the last half of the climb she stumbled along behind him praying it would end soon, badly winded when they reached the summit. Blake, though, hardly seemed affected.

How could that be? He worked in an office with computers, for God's sake. As for herself, all she wanted to do was throw herself down on the ground and gasp like a landed fish until the stitch in her side eased.

She dragged air into her lungs and tried to stop her legs from shaking like jelly. Tried not to huff and puff too loudly. Tried to keep her gaze from drifting back to Blake.

He hadn't had to deal with what she'd had to on that climb. Every time she'd glanced upwards, she'd been confronted with the most perfect backside man had ever had the fortune to be graced with. Which had absolutely nothing to do with her lack of air. She brought the picture to mind once more with remarkable precision—taut, firm and mouth-wateringly tempting. Okay, so maybe it had everything to do with it, but...

She clenched her hands. She would *not* think about Blake that way. Friends, that was what they were. That was *all* they were.

Gritting her teeth, she stared doggedly at the filtered water views. To be friends again...it was everything. Why mess with that? She couldn't deal with more grief this year, and she had no intention of courting it.

Recalling the panic on his face when he'd

thought the kiss had detrimentally affected their friendship, she forced her pulse to slow. He wasn't in any better frame of mind at the moment than her when it came to making big decisions. She didn't want to do anything to hurt him either. They both just needed to be...careful.

'You okay?'

She nodded without making eye contact. 'Just disgustingly unfit.'

He handed her a bottle of water from the small backpack he'd slung over one shoulder. 'That was a tough climb.'

'Not for you apparently.'

'I haven't been housebound looking after anyone for the last however long.'

Ten years, she inserted silently. Not that she'd been housebound for all of those years. Nor had she been an utter drudge. She'd had access to outside help when she'd needed it. Most days she'd had a chance to get out for a walk or a run.

He hitched his head at the path. 'I'm reliably informed that spectacular views are in this direction.'

'After that climb, there'd better be.' And they'd better be worth the effort. This time when she fell in line behind him, she kept her gaze firmly from his backside.

She studied the trees and tried to identify where the scents of pine, sun-warmed grasses and wildflowers came from; tried to spot the birds chattering and tweeting among the branches and bushes.

She was so busy concentrating on *not* staring at Blake's bottom that the view opened up when she least expected it to. She halted beside him, neither of them saying a word as they studied the grand vista of gloriously blue sea and dramatic coastline.

The view would be amazing on a grey day, but when the sun shone so brightly, as it did today, the scene throbbed with a brilliance that made her glad to be alive.

'Okay.' She nodded. 'That's definitely worth the climb. This has to be one of the most beautiful places on earth.'

Blake couldn't agree more. He glanced at Nina from the corner of his eyes and let out a slow breath.

Look after Nina.

I'm trying to, Gran. He set back along the path. Kissing Nina, though, hadn't been part of the plan. The thought of ruining their friendship forever…

Things clenched. Acid burned his stomach and his lungs cramped so hard breathing became damn near impossible. If he wasn't careful he'd be in the grip of the biggest panic attack he'd ever had. Except some of that clenching was thrilling too. The stolen kisses last night had been spectacular.

Their memory burned through his consciousness now, drawing his skin tight and making his groin throb. Maybe it was the forbidden aspect of their kisses—one *shouldn't* have carnal thoughts about their best friend. For God's sake, they'd known each other since they were four years old—Nina was practically a sister.

Except he'd *never* viewed her in a sisterly light.

One thing he did know, though, was that his life wouldn't feel whole without her.

Glancing back at her, he let out a slow breath. At least some of the awkwardness she'd desperately tried to hide during breakfast had started to melt away. He readjusted the backpack, his hands clenching around the straps. He would *stop* thinking about kissing Nina and get things back to normal between them.

In the meantime, it wouldn't hurt to give them both something different to occupy their minds with. Like what was Nina planning to do with her future?

He'd been holding the question back, wanting to give her a chance to relax and unwind before asking it. He suspected it was part of what Gran had meant when she'd asked him to *look after Nina.* But more to the point, he wanted to know. Not out of curiosity, but because he wanted to find out if he could do anything to help.

And because he cared.

Hands clenching and unclenching, he tracked a small bird that darted from tree to tree in front of them as if it were Puck leading them further and further into an enchanted forest. He went to laugh at himself for being so fanciful, but at the same time it hit him that, to date, he'd never dabbled in game design. But a bird leading the player deeper and deeper into a game could be a fun opening.

'Where did you just go?' Nina asked from behind him. 'You were miles away.'

He waited for her to draw up next to him, then pointed. 'See that little bird?'

'The common chiffchaff?'

How did she know its name? He shook himself. 'Anyway, I had a fanciful notion that it was a magical guide in an enchanted forest, but...'

She stared. 'But?'

He shrugged. 'Is it friend or foe?'

'Or it could just be a common chiffchaff.' Her hands went to her hips. 'Have you had too much sun, Blake?'

He laughed. 'I've not yet dabbled in designing computer games. I mean, every man and his dog has, so I've avoided it. But...' He glanced back at the little bird. 'That's where my mind just went to as I watched the *common chiffchaff.*'

Golden toffee eyes stared at him as if he'd just uttered something amazing. All of the things he'd previously tried to unclench clenched up again twice as tight. Forcing his feet forward, he dragged air into his lungs and kept his eyes straight ahead.

Kissing Nina beneath the stars in Monte Carlo had been amazing. But kissing her here in the brilliant sunlight in an enchanted glade in the most beautiful place on earth would be life-changing.

Think you're overreacting?

Maybe, but his every instinct told him it would be dangerous, and he heeded the warning. He wasn't messing with Nina that way. He'd hurt her enough this year—he wanted to prove himself worthy of her forgiveness, of her friendship. He wanted to give, not take. He *wasn't* his mother.

'You know what, Blake?'

He didn't turn to glance back at her. 'What?'

'I don't play computer games, not even Solitaire, but if you created that game—and so long as it wasn't some shoot-'em-up or series of epic battles involving swords and spears and longbows—I'd play it.'

He swung back. 'Really?'

She nodded. 'And there have to be other people like me who want gentler games where they get to explore gorgeous and/or strange worlds while working out the rules as they go along, and maybe solving a mystery or a puzzle.'

His mind immediately fired with possibilities. How long had it been since he'd been excited by anything work-related? His graphic design platform had been, and continued to be, a huge hit, but ever since it had been launched all he'd been working on were improvements and additions. He'd figured he was a one-hit wonder. But now...

A soft touch on his arm hauled him back. She stared up at him with a frown in her eyes and he shook himself. 'I keep finding myself asking the same question you did in Cannes. When did I become so stuffy?' When had he become so risk averse?

She gestured around. 'This isn't stuffy.'

'Neither was parasailing or splashing money at the gaming tables,' he agreed.

'Or dining on caviar with a Hollywood star.'

'I've done all of those things… And now my mind is firing with new ideas and I feel alive in a way I haven't in ages. I don't think it's a coincidence.'

She lifted her arms, let them drop again. 'Why aren't you having adventures and doing fun things with your life as well as working, Blake? You can do both.'

'I can't remember when I became all work and no play.'

He knew, though. Of course he knew. They'd halted while they spoke, but he set back off now. The path at this point wasn't wide enough for them to walk side by side and he was grateful for it.

'Yes, you do,' she said as if she could see inside his head. 'You've been all work and no play ever since your graphic design software took off and you became wealthy. You think splurging money on non-essential things like fun and adventures makes you an irresponsible spendthrift, that it's frivolous and makes you as bad as your parents.'

He grimaced.

'Which is stupid. And I'm hoping, as a relatively intelligent human being, you've started to realise that.'

'Jeez, Nina, don't hold back, will you?'

The wry twist of his lips made her laugh. 'Everyone needs a bit of fun in their lives, Blake. It doesn't have to cost anything. It can just be ambling down to the cricket pitch on a Sunday afternoon to cheer on the team, playing a game of pool at the pub, cooking up a batch of scones or a Victoria sponge to enter into the agricultural show in the hopes of winning a blue ribbon.'

She made it sound easy.

'What do you do for fun at home, Blake?'

'Work.' He worked a lot.

'In an ideal world everyone would get a sense of satisfaction from their job. But at the end of the day, work is work.'

'There's a climbing wall at my local gym. That's kind of fun. I'm getting better at it.' He'd been pushing himself harder and harder in recent months.

'Which answers that question,' she said, almost to herself. 'Do you go out for dinner—dancing…? To see a game of football or a show?'

He did a bit of schmoozing for work, but that wasn't relaxing. He occasionally caught up with his friends from his university days, but only one of them was currently living in London. 'Maybe I've been taking the lone-wolf thing a bit too far,' he admitted, wanting to bring the conversation to a close. They shouldn't be focusing on him. They should be focusing on her.

'You think?'

It struck him that he'd been all at sea without her this year. Chatting to her had always been fun, but it had also kept him grounded. Why had he let that silence between them go on for so long? All he could do now was try to mend the damage he'd unwittingly caused. 'Right, your turn.'

'I have fun.'

'You do,' he agreed, even if he secretly thought line dancing the antithesis of fun. 'What I've been wanting to ask, though, is what are your plans for the future?'

'Oh.' Her voice sounded suddenly flat. He glanced back to see her wrinkle her nose at a grove of pine trees. 'I don't know yet. I haven't worked it out.'

Maybe he could help with that. But he let the matter drop as he followed the map directions to a lookout. They stared in awe at the colour of the water—so blue—and the picturesque inlet that housed the monastery far below.

They didn't talk much after that, but as they reached the last leg of the hike, he blew out a breath. 'The descent is a series of steep switch-backs.'

She peered around his shoulder. 'Yikes, I'll be taking this slow.'

They were three quarters of the way down when

Nina gave a muted yelp. He spun to find her sliding on her backside towards him. In one smooth motion, he wrapped a hand around a nearby tree branch to anchor himself before scooping an arm around her and lifting her upright again. 'Okay?'

Her hands landed on his chest, her breaths coming short and fast. 'Fine. Bruised pride, nothing more.'

Their gazes collided and he swore that when those eyes, the colour of maple syrup, lowered to his mouth and her pupils dilated, that sweetness exploded on his tongue. The raw hunger that momentarily flared across her face jolted through him like lightning. A longing so intense gripped him that he felt as if he were hurtling down a wicked ravine with no end in sight.

Nina *wanted* him. She wanted him every bit as much as he wanted her. His pulse pounded and something in his chest lightened and tightened at the same time. He—

She blinked and shot away so fast he had to grab her arms to keep her upright. As soon as she had her balance again, he released her and swung back to the front. Bile burned his throat and his heart pounded like a wild thing. They weren't doing that, remember? Sex complicated everything. Her friendship meant way too much to risk it all on a short-term fling.

You sure about that?

Gritting his teeth, he nodded. *Positive.*

He didn't get his pulse back under control until they'd been served coffee and Italian cream cake at a tiny café overlooking the pebbly beach at San Fruttuoso Abbey. 'You want to tour the abbey?'

Her eyes brightened. 'Yes, please!'

He grinned at the speed of her reply. She seemed just as excited about that as she had about a night at the casino. Maybe that was the key to rejigging his life—to approach everything with enthusiasm.

'Want to catch the ferry back to Portofino rather than retrace our steps?'

'Yes, please,' she said even more quickly and with even more emphasis, and they both laughed. And just like that things were right again. He'd missed this—missed the camaraderie and the sense of… Belonging he supposed. Nina just got him. He *wouldn't* ruin things again. He couldn't.

'So tell me the options.'

She glanced up. Cream from her cake had smeared her lips and he could've groaned out loud when she licked it off. He shovelled cake into his mouth. *Taste the cake. Chew the cake. Focus on the cake.*

'Options for what?' She sipped her coffee while she waited for him to finish his mouthful. 'Man, I love Italian coffee.' She took another quick sip before setting her cup down.

He tried to pull himself together. 'The options you're considering for your future.'

Her face fell and he regretted asking. Maybe he

should let the matter drop and let her enjoy the holiday. But she'd eventually have to turn her mind to it. And if there was anything he could do to help...

'Well, Sara Mackie, the manager of the nursing home, has offered me a job as an enrolled nurse.'

He did what he could to stop his nose from curling. 'Is that what you want to do?'

Her shrug said it all, though he doubted she was aware of it.

'I'm glad I was able to spend so much time with Mum and Granny Day. It was a privilege. I like caring for people, Blake, and I'm good at it.'

'But?'

'No buts.' She bit her lip, one shoulder lifting. 'Okay, maybe I'm a bit tired of it. Maybe I'd like to try my hand at something different, but...*what*?'

'You could go to uni.' She'd always wanted to do that.

'To do *what*? To study *what*?'

'Or you could come to London and work for Drawing Board.'

'Your company? As *what*? I'm not qualified for anything. And also...' She pointed her cake fork at him. 'Nepotism, much?'

'You could try a few different things at the company—HR, PR, admin—and see what you liked.'

'I'm not taking handouts.'

'I'd love it, though, if you came to London, Nina.' And if he could entice her with the promise of a job...

Toffee eyes speared his. He swallowed, refusing to allow the moment to develop and deepen into anything *more*. 'What do you love doing besides line dancing?'

She rolled her eyes. 'Well, apart from my garden, and the occasional baking session in the kitchen, and catching up with friends...' She trailed off with a shrug.

Her garden! He straightened. Why hadn't he thought of that? 'I remember you saying you wanted to be an environmental scientist of some kind when we were kids.' A dream she'd buried when she'd realised how much help her mum had needed. 'You were forever talking about wanting to take care of the planet. You were Callenbrook's very own environmental crusader.' That was a dream she could resurrect now.

'Yeah, but that was like a million years ago.'

'You're not thirty yet, Nina. Stop acting like an old lady. It's not too late to do something new, something you'd love. It's not too late to make a difference.'

CHAPTER EIGHT

IT'S NOT TOO late to make a difference.

Nina pulled her white towelling robe more securely about her as she moved to the yacht's stern on the lower deck and stared out at the moonlight reflected on the water. Not even the tiniest of breezes disturbed its surface. It looked soft and inviting…and maybe even promising the freedom Iris claimed for it. She glanced at the moon that hung huge in the sky. Full tonight. Full moons had a strange power, didn't they? Maybe that was why Blake's words continued to play in her mind.

It's not too late to make a difference.

She'd already made a difference, and he'd be the first to acknowledge it, but she also knew that wasn't what he'd meant. When they were in high school she'd used to brag that she'd make a difference on a global scale. Not in a famous, everyone-knew-her-name kind of way. She'd just wanted to make a deep and significant difference to the natural world. She'd wanted to preserve and protect the environment, to do all she could to live sustainably, and to teach others how to live more sustainably too.

How could she have forgotten that dream?

She grimaced into the night. Because to dwell on it would've perhaps generated feelings of resentment, a sense of being left behind by her peers, a hint of bitterness, and she hadn't wanted to be that person. Neither her mother nor Iris had asked her to take on the role of their carer. She'd *chosen* to do it. She'd wanted to embrace her decision wholeheartedly, with grace and generosity...and not with a tiny prickly burr of 'what if' buried deep inside her heart.

She didn't regret the choices she'd made. She was proud of the way she'd dealt with all of it.

She winced. Okay, nearly all of it. She wasn't necessarily proud of the way she'd cut Blake loose as she had. She should've given him a chance to explain—she should've taken his calls.

In her defence, she'd been dealing with a lot. So she wasn't going to beat herself up about it too much. He'd been dealing with a lot too, though, and she didn't want him beating up on himself either. They'd both made mistakes. But they were restoring their friendship, fixing it and making it strong once more. And if he came home for Christmas...

Don't get your hopes up. Even if he meant every word, even if she didn't continue to have question marks in her mind, the man was a big deal these days. A billionaire! He had responsibilities that could call him away at a moment's notice.

Anyway, it was time to stop thinking—*brooding*—about Blake. That wasn't what she was up here on deck to do. Climbing the ladder down to the platform that housed the inflatable motorboat, she shrugged off her robe and sat beside it to dangle her legs in the water. The water temperature was a very pleasant twenty degrees Celsius.

'Okay, Granny Day... Let's do this.' Slipping *silently* into the water—she didn't want to alert anyone to what she was up to—she took a few experimental strokes away from the yacht before moving back and removing her bikini top and tossing it up onto the platform. Her bottoms followed shortly afterwards.

Oh my God. She was naked—completely and utterly. She swam a few strokes of freestyle... and then breaststroke, before turning on her back to stare at the moon. *Hot damn.* Iris was right—skinny-dipping was a sensory experience definitely worth having. With nothing between her and the sea—she closed her eyes to relish the feeling—she'd never felt so unfettered. She gave a soft laugh. It felt extraordinary and she wondered now why she'd been so worried about it. Why—

'*What* are you doing?'

She gave a muffled scream and immediately jackknifed into a vertical position so *nothing* peeked out of the water other than her head.

Blake. Oh, God.

He made his way down to the lower platform. Reaching down, he picked up her bikini. His jaw sagged. 'You aren't?'

Something in his tone made her chin lift. 'I am.'

Both his jaw and his fist clenched, the gold bikini glittering between his fingers like stardust, and he shook it at her. 'You have to be joking me.'

She dog-paddled a little closer so they could keep their voices low. '*I* am skinny-dipping because *I* am not stuffy or hung up on what people might say about me behind my back. *I*, for one, am young and free enough to enjoy every new experience that comes my way without being tied in knots by convention.'

His hands slammed to his hips. 'Have you been drinking?'

'Seriously?' She rolled her eyes. 'I'm skinny-dipping, Blake. *Not* stupid. Midnight swims and drinking don't seem like a particularly good combination.'

He pointed a shaking finger at her. 'This can't be legal.'

She shrugged, careful to make sure everything that mattered stayed below the water. 'Europeans are far more relaxed about nudity than Australians.'

'You could get us *arrested*.'

'Well, as *you* aren't the one skinny-dipping, I'm thinking you'll be fine. So turn around and walk away and stop spoiling my fun.'

Not a single muscle moved and yet hurt still somehow managed to radiate from him. Her heart slipped to her toes and then sank down to the bottom of the sea. *Oh, Blake.* She ached for him. Ever since his parents had been arrested he'd refused to step a foot outside the rigid boundaries he'd set for himself—holding himself to impossible standards.

She refused to let her chin drop. 'Or you could stop your bellyaching and join me.'

Her words made him blink. Was that yearning that crept across his face? A part of her wanted to cry for him. He didn't need to hold himself such a prisoner. He should be able to let his hair down and live a little.

'Blake...'

His gaze speared back to hers.

'I dare you.'

His eyes narrowed. In the next moment his shirt came over his head and he stepped out of his shorts. He stood before her in nothing but a pair of briefs and it was her turn to get choked up. The man truly did have the most magnificent physique.

With a superhuman effort, she found her voice, and lifted an arm out of the water to point at him. '*Fully* naked,' she ordered, spinning around when his hands went to his briefs, although turning around and not looking was one of the hardest things she'd ever done. It shocked her how much she wanted to see all of him—all of him *naked.*

A soft splash informed her that he'd dived into

the water. From just behind her, he said, 'You can spare your maidenly blushes, Nina. It's safe to turn around. I'm in the water.'

Did he think her unnecessarily prim? She turned and tried for blasé. 'I thought it polite to give you some privacy. It seemed voyeuristic to watch when…' she shrugged '…well, when that's not what this is about. So,' she rushed on before he could say anything, 'before things get weird between us, turn your back to me, float a little, stare up at the sky at all of those stars, and feel the water against your skin. *Really* feel it… Maybe swim a little. It feels… Well, I haven't fully worked that out yet, so if and when you do, let me know.'

He followed her instructions. She tried not to watch, though she might as well have tried to stop the tide. The temptation was too great. Besides, it wasn't as if she could *see* anything.

But knowing what was just below the surface of the water, so close to her…

He turned, making her blink. 'It's extraordinary,' he finally said.

She smiled at the frown in his voice. 'I know! Who knew?'

She relaxed then too. They swam—sort of together and sort of apart—they floated. She eventually sensed him moving closer, but kept her gaze on the stars. One large warm hand wrapped around hers and he threaded their fingers together. 'I'm never going to forget this.'

'Me either.' She turned her head and smiled. 'If I was a billionaire, I'd buy a private beach and skinny-dip whenever I wanted.'

He grinned. 'You want me to buy you a private beach?'

She laughed, stifling a yawn at the same time. 'I want you to buy yourself a beach and do this as often as you can.'

'Will you come visit?'

'Try and stop me.'

He hitched his head in the direction of the yacht. 'Time to head in?'

She nodded and they moved back to the boat. Nina grimaced. 'Okay, here's where it gets awkward, because I don't actually want anyone to see me naked.'

His gaze darkened, deepened. 'While right now there's nothing I want more on this earth.'

Their gazes collided and clashed. Her mouth dried. Everything clenched.

'However, I'll play the hero.' Resting his palms on the platform, he sent her a sidelong glance. 'I'm going up, so if you don't want to see me naked…'

Oh, but she did. She *really* did. Clapping a hand over her eyes, she spun around, her heart in her mouth at the sounds of splashing and dripping behind her, at the sound of his feet padding across the deck.

'Okay, I'm decent.'

She turned back to find him wearing his shorts,

but nothing else. He hadn't towelled off—because he hadn't brought a towel…because he hadn't expected to go swimming. *Skinny-dipping.*

Water beaded his skin, that tanned chest and those broad shoulders gleamed in the silver glow of the moon and she wanted to explore the planes of that big body with her hands and her mouth and—

Stop it!

What, you've gone skinny-dipping and now lost all control of yourself?

It should sound crazy, but in swimming naked in the sea it felt as if she'd thrown off invisible shackles that she hadn't known had been binding her.

Seizing her robe, he shook it at her. As if trying to shake her to her senses. But she couldn't help thinking it was more like waving a red flag at a bull. Or waving a white flag of surrender. That last thought had the pulse surging in her throat. She'd surrendered to the sea and it had been amazing… wonderful. If she and Blake surrendered to their attraction…

The taut expression on his face crashed her back into the present.

He held out the robe, his gaze angled up and staring—*glaring*—skywards. 'Not taking my eyes off the moon, Nina. So any time you're ready…'

Her arms felt rubbery but she hauled herself up onto the platform and moved across on unsteady legs to pluck the robe from his fingers. Pushing her arms through the sleeves, she tied the belt securely around her waist. 'Let's go.'

Without looking at him, she climbed the short ladder to the main deck and started for the door. 'I'm going to grab a cold water. Would you like one too?'

She glanced over her shoulder to find Blake's gaze glued to her backside. The dark, heated expression in his eyes when he lifted them to her face had the blood rushing to the surface of her skin making her hot and prickly and so aware of him she wanted to scream. 'Water, Blake?' she croaked.

'You haven't had enough of the stuff for one night?'

Her throat dried. 'I'm parched.'

Their words were saying one thing, but their eyes and the rest of their bodies were saying something else entirely. Dear God, this was crazy. She needed to leave *now*.

She swung away, taking another two steps to reach the door. If she walked through it, some invisible thread stretching between her and Blake would snap. Snapping it would be the sensible thing to do, but she...

She swallowed. She didn't want to break it.

Turning, she met his gaze again. One beat passed. Then another.

At exactly the same moment, they took a step towards one another. Above them that benevolent, cunning moon continued to glow, casting a silver light upon everything. Blake's hunger was plain for her to see—he wanted her with an intensity that stole her breath. It was laced with a hint of confusion and a dose of concern and she knew her face mirrored the exact same expression.

Neither of them tried to hide it. What was the point? They knew each other too well. Could read each other so well. 'So here's the thing, Blake. I want to see you naked too.'

'I know.'

'This is crazy,' she whispered.

'Totally. But hot.'

His words raked across her skin, raising gooseflesh and pebbling her nipples to hard aching peaks. 'Smoking hot,' she groaned.

'Too crazy?'

It was a question not a statement. He was asking her if she thought they ought to act on this. Or if they should walk away from it. He'd accept her decision. She knew he would. But he was making his own position clear—he wanted her, and he had no intention of walking away from it unless she asked him to.

It was comforting to find then that she couldn't. She hitched up her chin. 'Our friendship has survived a lot.'

'It has.'

'I can't see any reason why it wouldn't also survive a temporary friends-with-benefits arrangement, can you?'

He swallowed. She had a feeling his mouth had gone as dry as hers.

'I mean, you're wedded to your lone-wolf status while I'm...' she lifted her shoulders in a shrug '...in transition and not interested in falling in love with anyone at the moment.' There'd be no point. She wanted to live a little before settling down.

'So you're saying...?'

'You and me...and a temporary Mediterranean fling.'

A bead of water dripped from the end of his hair to slide down his neck and then along his collarbone—trembled there for a moment, before spilling over to track a path down his chest towards his navel. Her breathing grew more laboured.

'Nina?'

Her name was a groan and she lifted eyes heavy with desire. 'I dare you.'

Fire flashed in his eyes. Reaching across, he caught her chin in firm fingers and his lips landed on hers and he kissed her with such an innate sensuality it had her melting against him, her hands splaying against his chest and relishing the heat and firmness of the muscles beneath her palms.

'Challenge accepted,' he murmured against her lips.

Her lips curved into a smile, and, taking his hand, she led him down to her cabin. Dropping his hand once they were inside, she strode into the en-suite bathroom to return with a box of condoms that she tossed onto the bed.

He stared at the box and then at her. 'There's a reason we're such good friends.'

She nodded. And then untied the sash of her robe and let it fall off her shoulders to pool at her feet.

His swift intake of breath—the flaring nostrils, the darkening of his eyes, the parting of his lips— all arrowed to her core. With slow measured steps, he moved across to her. Nothing felt rushed now, nothing felt urgent, but the very air was pregnant with promise.

'Beautiful,' he breathed. 'And now I'm having the most intense fantasy.'

His gaze held hers. Her pulse throbbed, skipped, danced. 'Tell me.'

His gaze lowered to linger on her breasts, and they immediately tingled to life. His gaze travelled further south to the curve of her waist and then the juncture of her thighs. She could feel herself melting and yearning and he hadn't even touched her yet.

Those brilliant blue eyes lifted back to her face. 'I'm imagining myself buried inside you, all of your muscles clenching around me as you come screaming my name.'

As he spoke, he undid the button at the waistband of his shorts, lowered the zip and let them drop to the floor, where he stepped out of them. She followed his movement with her gaze and took in the size of him—the length and girth of his erection.

Catching her bottom lip between her teeth, she glanced up, not even trying to hide her smile. 'Oh, my.'

One corner of his mouth hooked up. Reaching up, she drew his head down to hers. 'How about we see if we can make this fantasy of yours come true?'

They kissed with a lazy, laconic joy—as if they had all the time in the world. As if they were in the right place at the right time and they meant to make the very most of it.

But the heat and need—the naked roaring hunger—refused to be suppressed. They explored each other's bodies with a greedy, hungry possessiveness. Blake kissed every inch of her. Until she was a mindless, writhing mass of sensation. Their bodies slid together with a knowing ease—as if they'd done this before…as if their bodies had minds and wills of their own, while they themselves simply held on for the ride.

His warm firm flesh against hers. His hardness inside her. His hands moving and moulding, teasing, pulling her closer. It had the pressure and the pleasure building in ever tighter and more intense concentric circles until, with a scream, she peaked and hurtled into an abyss of gold-flecked pleasure that went on and on, and gave and gave, until it both emptied and filled her utterly. Vaguely she was aware of Blake's joyous shout joining hers. And the slow, peaceful floating that followed afterwards.

She didn't know if minutes had passed or hours or an eternity when she eventually turned her head on the pillow. Blake turned his head too.

Neither of them spoke. Eventually Blake swore. A word so rude it startled a laugh from her. But he'd uttered it so softly and sweetly it sounded like an endearment. She nodded. 'That was really... something.'

'Momentous.'

'Earth-shattering.'

It was a game they played. And his mouth hooked up. 'Stellar.'

'A revelation.'

He met her gaze, his lips pursing. 'A mistake?'

His sudden stillness had things inside her drawing tight, but she sensed the hidden fear behind his words and shook her head. 'I don't think so. I mean, if it is, it's one I want to repeat.' Over and over.

His tension dissolved and he feigned a nonchalant shrug. 'I suppose we could always try it again just to make sure.'

She did what she could to suppress a grin. 'Excellent idea.'

How could it be a mistake? They knew each other too well for misunderstandings. They knew exactly what to expect from one another.

You were expecting that?

Well, no. But it had been out of this world, and she wasn't giving that experience back for anything.

She laughed when, quick as a flash, Blake rolled her over and pinned her to the bed. 'Now, before we get distracted again, where should I tell our skipper to set sail for in the morning?'

'Nowhere. I want to stay in Portofino forever.'

His grin, when it came, curled her toes. 'Let's call that Plan A, then.'

She rolled him over then until she could straddle him. 'I now have a fantasy of my own to tell you about.'

His hands shaped her waist and hips. 'I'm all ears.'

They slept late—needing the rest after the exertions of the night before. To the chef's delight they demolished their breakfast with gusto. And then to the deckhand's delight—and Nina's, which was the point of the exercise after all—Blake ordered the waterslide to be set up. It was a huge inflatable number that one accessed via the sky lounge. Nina's whoops of delight as she tried it out, sliding into the blue water far below, made him feel ten years younger.

Maybe twenty years!

The thought had him immediately shaking his head. He might've had an enthusiasm for slides and slippery dips as a ten-year-old but he sure as hell hadn't felt about any girl the way he did for Nina now. That emotion was strictly adult.

He stole kisses from her as they floated in the sea. She stole teasing, tempting touches. He couldn't believe how good it felt to have her in his life again. He couldn't believe how good it felt to be whole again.

He'd been an idiot not to tell her about his panic attacks immediately, an idiot for feeling embarrassed and small because of them. And he'd been an idiot to stay away for so long. He swore he'd never again do anything like that, never again risk their friendship.

To not have Nina in his life… The thought made no sense. In a very real way, Nina had been his anchor since he'd been four years old. He couldn't imagine his life without her. He didn't want to.

Then what are you doing messing with her like this?

The thought slid beneath his guard—a sliver of ice piercing his heart.

Don't be silly. This fling was consensual—a bit of fun after all the hardship and grief. Once they left this enchanted place, once their Mediterranean holiday was at an end, they'd return to their individual homes on opposite sides of the world and their friendship would return to normal.

Normal?

He glared at the water. All friendships evolved,

went through different phases. When they returned to the real world, theirs would emerge even deeper and stronger than before.

No more sex?

What the hell…? *No! No more sex once they returned home.*

Sex with Nina when they returned to their everyday worlds couldn't happen. *That* would ruin everything. He didn't do commitment, Nina knew that, but if they were to continue to mess around like this when they returned home, it might give her the impression that he'd changed his mind.

A chill chased down his spine. Not *ever* going to happen. He had no intention of handing any woman the same power that his mother had wielded over him and his father. Not even Nina. He *cherished* his lone-wolf status.

Splashing water over his face, he dashed it from his eyes and dragged in a deep breath to try and slow the sudden racing of his heart. Of all the women he knew, Nina was the one woman who'd have the power to bind him to her will. She'd always been able to talk him into anything. One day it'd be skinny-dipping, and the next it'd be…robbing a bank!

Nina a bank robber? Seriously?

He rolled his shoulders. Fine, maybe he was exaggerating, but he knew what he meant. It'd be smaller scale, not so dramatic—wanting him to change jobs, to move house, to move to a different country. And just… *No.* They *weren't* going to dance that dance. He'd be the driver of his own life, thank you very much.

Diving under the water, he swam as far as he could until burning lungs forced him back to the surface. It helped to knock some sense back into him. He was creating monsters out of shadows. Nina wasn't interested in their relationship deepening into anything more.

How had she phrased it? She was *in transition.* She wasn't sure yet what she wanted to do with her life. She wanted to work that out, have a chance to follow her own dreams before becoming involved with anyone. Smart. Sensible. It was one of the reasons they got on so well.

He turned at her shout to see her launch herself once more down the water slide. And having the time of her life. He grinned and swam towards her. She deserved every drop of fun, every shot of delight, that came her way. And he'd do everything in his power to facilitate it.

Swimming over to him, she slipped behind him to wrap one arm around his shoulders and the other about his waist, her hands splaying against his chest and abdomen, sparking heat and need in their wake.

'Blake?'

Her breath against his ear had him humming. 'Hmm?'

'You don't happen to have a jet-ski licence, do you?'

She pressed herself against his back and he swore stars burst behind his eyelids. 'I do.' Though if he hadn't, he'd have sworn to get one by the close of business that day if that was what she wanted. She swam around in front of him, her smile huge and eyes bright. The heat in his veins didn't dissipate, but a surge of tenderness rushed to join it.

'Really?'

'I know that, given my stuffy tendencies, it's out of character, but a while back I was invited to an investor's beachy paradise and advised to get a jet-ski licence prior to attending.'

Her hands went to his shoulders and his automatically went to her waist. Their legs tangled in the most tantalising fashion. 'You weren't too stuffy last night when you had me screaming out your name.'

All of his blood rushed to his groin. 'God, Nina, are you trying to drown me?'

'Absolutely not. I have plans for you later— wicked plans.'

She waggled her eyebrows like some pantomime villain and he couldn't help but laugh. 'Why'd you want to know about the jet-ski licence?'

'Apparently we have to have a licence to operate one. If not, then one of the staff will take us out. But I don't want to hold onto George. I want to hold onto you.'

Him and Nina zipping across the water, her holding on tight behind and whooping into the breeze? Sign him up!

'So I was hoping later on this afternoon maybe we could do that? After lunch. And an, um, afternoon...nap.'

The mischief in her eyes told him *napping* wasn't what she had in mind.

'I can't think of anything I'd rather do.'

Her grin, her delight, and the easing of some innate tension—partly grief and, he suspected, partly the weight of all the things she'd had to deal with over the last few months—were his reward. He swore in that moment to do everything that he could to help that tension disappear entirely.

'So tell me about the skinny-dipping.'

Nina glanced across at him, took a sip of the *very* nice Sémillon he'd selected from the cellar. Dinner on the yacht this evening had allowed them to remain encased in their own private bubble, and had capped off a perfect day. The lights of Portofino curved away to Blake's right, and directly out in front of him the moon made a path of silver on the dark water.

'This place is magic,' she murmured, before shuffling upright a little. 'What do you mean, tell you about the skinny-dipping? What do you want to know?'

'Just *why*? What possessed you to do it in the

first place? Is it some secret yearning you've always had?' Did she have more secret yearnings he could help her fulfil? 'I just never in a million years would've guessed.'

Her laugh washed over him like a caress. 'Totally out of character,' she agreed. 'As was the bikini on the beach in Cannes, the parasailing in Nice, and the gambling in Monte Carlo.'

Her lips curved into a smile so full of affection it made his heart beat harder. If she ever smiled at him like that...

Friendship, that was what this was. That was all it was ever going to be. *Don't forget it.*

'Iris has been leaving me instructions—a challenge for each of the destinations on our itinerary.'

'No way.'

'She says I need a shake-up—wants to push me out of my comfort zone.'

'Wow.' No wonder she'd been so intent on the parasailing. No wonder she'd been determined to enjoy the beach in Cannes.

'And it's worked. I mean, I'm still sad because she and Mum are no longer with us, but...' her hands lifted '...it's reminded me that there's a big wide world out there. It's shown me that I can still have fun.' She was silent for several long moments. 'I've spent most of my time this last couple of years with older people—senior citizens—and this trip has reminded me that I'm still young.'

'And beautiful, desirable, smart and funny. And the best friend a person could ever have.'

She stared at him. Her smile when it came was full of affection, and this time it was directed wholly at him. It made his heart beat harder than it ever had before.

'Ah, but, Blake, *you're* the one who has shown me all of those things and made me believe them.'

Her words, the expression in her eyes, choked him up. He did his best to make light of it. 'Go me!'

She laughed, but sobered a moment later. 'I'm glad we took this trip together.'

So was he—to the depths of his soul.

'Now...' she leaned towards him '...my next challenge from Iris isn't until Positano...'

'Are you eager to read it?'

'Absolutely.'

'Do you want to head for the Amalfi Coast tomorrow, then?'

'Absolutely not. There's no rush. Besides, Iris told us to add a couple of other stops to our itinerary. Is there anywhere you'd like to go?'

'The Cinque Terre,' he answered promptly. 'You?'

'Corfu.'

Excellent. It meant the trip wouldn't end any time soon. He lifted his glass in a toast. 'Trip of a lifetime!'

She touched her glass to his with a grin.

CHAPTER NINE

NINA AND BLAKE spent another day in Portofino, and Nina swore it was her new best favourite place. While the beauty of Portofino was jaw-dropping, awe-inspiring and soul-soothing, it was the beauty of her travelling companion that held her spellbound.

Blake. The wry humour, intelligence and generosity of the boy she'd known growing up was still there, but now inside a grown man's body— a *hot* male body. It made him both a known and unknown quantity. It added an edge to all of their interactions—a thrilling edge that held a tiny hint of danger.

Danger? She snorted. She wasn't in danger from Blake. This *release*—because that was what it felt like, a release—was simply the relief from the oppressive cloud of grief that had smothered her world and held her prisoner for this last year. Watching her mum waste away and lose her battle with the disease she'd fought for nearly two decades had damn well broken her heart. To then repeat that experience with Iris... She dragged in a breath and released it slowly. It had left her feeling dejected and lonely and bleak.

As Iris had hoped, though, this trip had reminded Nina that there was more to life—fine and exciting things that she could embrace. Instead of a flat grey future, promises like jewels now gleamed on the horizon.

She could be an environmental scientist, an ecologist. She could travel the world with those qualifications, and the world could be her garden. The thought put the biggest smile on her face.

As did this adventure she'd embarked on with Blake. How many women could boast a hot fling in the Mediterranean? The fact that she could had her feeling like a brand-new person.

Not in a million years would she have thought she and Blake would become lovers. If he'd remained in Callenbrook, she doubted it would've happened—familiarity breeding contempt and all that. But seeing Blake on a video call didn't have the same impact as seeing the man in the flesh. For this moment in time, she meant to make the most of it.

What about when all of this is over?

'What do we think about Christmas in Portofino in three years' time?' She slid a glance to the man beside her as he scattered a sprinkling of Iris's ashes into the bay before they set sail for the next leg of the journey. 'Callenbrook, then London, then Portofino.'

'It's a date.'

He said it so promptly it made her laugh.

When this was over, they'd go back to being the best of friends. Piece of cake. A part of her, though, winced at the assumed glibness. Would it really be that easy?

She frowned at the water. Why not? He'd be back in London. She'd be in Callenbrook—actually, she hoped she'd be at university in Melbourne—and their real-life realities would take over, and this holiday would become nothing more than a happy memory.

You could make more memories.

And they would. Memories of the *friendly* variety. Memories that weren't *sexy*. Their friendship had survived a lot. It could survive this too.

'You're looking unusually serious.'

She glanced up to find Blake watching her with a frown. She sent him a swift smile. 'I was thinking about us.'

They moved across to the sun loungers and stretched out.

'You're worried?' he said.

'Not really.'

His brows shot up. 'Not really?'

He homed in on her words like a radar on an approaching missile and she couldn't help but laugh. 'It's just, when this is at an end—' she gestured between them '—there'll have to be a bit of rene-gotiation.'

'I see.'

Her brows lifted. 'You do?'

He tapped a hand against his thigh and gri-maced. 'Sorry, I haven't a clue what you're talk-ing about.'

She huffed out a laugh. 'This holiday has been heaven—perfect—and I don't want it to end.'

He shrugged. 'We can extend it.'

'As tempting as that thought is, eventually we'll have to return to the real world. And when that happens…'

Leaning across, he took her hand. 'When that happens…?'

'I just think there ought to be some ground rules.'

'Okay. What kind of ground rules?'

His eyes informed her that he'd give her what-ever she wanted or die in the trying. A lump lodged in her throat and she had to blink hard.

He'll give you everything you want, except his love.

She blinked. What on earth…? She didn't *want* his love. She wasn't interested in commitment at the moment—this was me-time, remember? Blake loved her like a friend. That was enough.

You sure?

Of course she was sure.

'So you'll be in London and I'll be in Callenbrook, which means we won't be tempted to tumble into bed together whenever we clap eyes on each other.'

'Because we won't actually be clapping eyes on each other.'

'Exactly. But there'll be video calls.'

'Lots of those.'

'And they can't be...*flirty*?'

'Ah.' Comprehension dawned in those blue eyes.

'And when you come home for Christmas, there can't be any tumbling into bed together.'

He shifted on his seat. 'Of course not.'

'If we let this bleed into our real lives, that's when things could get complicated. I think we ought to avoid that.'

His nostrils flared. 'I don't want to do anything to hurt our friendship.'

'I know.' Nor did she.

She frowned as another thought occurred to her. 'Also, if you return to London and immediately fall in love with someone, perhaps don't tell me about it straight away. Wait until some time next year. I've never considered myself particularly possessive or jealous, but—'

Blake's laughter cut off the rest of her words. 'Never going to happen.'

The thought of him with another woman, though, screwed her up tight.

'Lone wolf, remember?'

Her tension didn't ease. She stared at him for

a long moment. 'Do you really not want to fall in love, though? Do you really not want to have children?'

His laughter bled away and his expression sobered. 'The latter isn't completely dependent on the former.'

She supposed not.

'But I definitely don't want the former.'

Her heart ached. His mother had done such a number on him.

'Though you do?'

'Absolutely. Eventually.' Not quite yet, though. She deserved some time to focus only on herself. Reaching for her hat, she plonked it on her head. 'One day I'd like the whole kit and caboodle— marriage, kids, the white picket fence, rowdy birthday parties, summer holidays at the seaside.' She stared out at the horizon. 'I want to do a lot with my life, Blake, but I want someone there beside me to do it with. To celebrate the good times with and a hand to hold in the hard times.'

'And what if this mystery man of yours—this paragon of virtue—lets you down like your father did?'

This argument was a familiar one from their younger days. 'What if he doesn't?'

He glared at the spectacular coastline as it slid past, his nose curling, and she started to laugh. 'If I return home and promptly fall in love, I won't mention it to you until some time next year either.

I know you're neither the possessive nor jealous type, but—'

'No!' He swung back to her so fast it made her blink. 'You *have* to tell me. *Immediately!* So I can come home and talk you out of it.'

She lowered her sunnies to stare at him over their rim. Her heart picking up speed.

'You have your whole life ahead of you, Nina. You have a chance to focus exactly on what *you* want for once. Don't waste it on some guy.'

Which was the same advice she'd been giving herself. And it was *good* advice.

They settled back on the sun loungers. 'Also, if any guy hurts you I'll break his neck.'

She laughed. 'It's nice having you in my corner again, Blake.'

'I plan to stay there.'

Good. 'In the meantime… Wanna join me in the hot tub?'

His face cleared. 'I thought you'd never ask.'

A wicked light gleamed in those blue eyes and her veins heated instantly. Today was a good day. At the moment, that was all she needed to focus on.

They spent several days exploring the Cinque Terre, with its terraced slopes, picturesque pastel houses and glorious views. They ate figs and dined on fresh fish. They sipped Aperol spritzes in the sun, swam in the warm sea…and gloried in their lovemaking.

Eventually, they sailed into the bay at Positano,

a playful breeze at their backs. Blake smiled down at her from their spot at the bow. 'Sick of glorious scenery yet?'

'Not a chance.' Why had she not known that the Italian coastline was so unrelentingly beautiful? Her guidebook informed her that the Amalfi Coast was considered one of the most beautiful coastlines in the world. As she stared at the vertical town rising up the steep hillside before her, colourful houses perched on cliffs, she could see her guidebook had a point. What a sight.

She stared and stared. Eventually she excused herself to race down to her cabin to open the envelope marked Positano.

'Look, Nina, I don't think this bar is any better than the last one. It's crowded and busy and—'

'It's not as busy as the first one and it's a little more, uh, refined than the second.'

'But—'

'No buts. I'm doing this.' Pulling in a breath, she released it slowly. Blake had vetoed the first two venues. She wasn't letting him veto a third. 'I think you should just go back to the boat.'

'No way.' He thrust out his jaw, his blue eyes glittering like a tropical thunderstorm and his hands slamming his hands to his hips. 'Gran really wants you to go into some bar and start a conversation with *a stranger*?'

As far as Nina was concerned, it was the easiest

of the challenges so far. Judging by Blake's reaction, he considered it the riskiest. She folded her arms and stuck out a hip. 'If you come in with me, it'll defeat the purpose.'

'What purpose?'

'To prove that I can stand on my own two feet and hold my own in a foreign country. This challenge—' like all of the challenges so far '—is designed to increase my confidence.'

He shoved his hands in his pockets, hooded eyes searching her face. 'Fine, but there's no harm in me going in there as well and keeping an eye on you from the bar.'

She wasn't some child or damsel who couldn't look after herself. *Fine*. 'If you come into that bar then you have to do the challenge as well.'

'*Me?* I—'

'For me, this is an easy challenge. For you, not so much.' She touched a hand to her chest. '*I* like meeting new people. *I* like talking to people.'

'So do I!'

'You big fat liar! Lone wolf, remember? You pride yourself on being the strong, silent type.' Before he could respond, she said, 'Here's the drill. I'm going into that bar and you're going to sit on this bench here for ten minutes before you follow me in.'

'And what? Twiddle my thumbs?'

'Admire the view; soak up the atmosphere.'

He rolled his shoulders at her pointed glare.

'Fine. But we need a signal for if you want me to wade in and rescue you.'

For heaven's sake… Gritting her teeth, she counted to five. 'Okay, fine. If I pull my hair back into a ponytail, that means I need rescuing. Deal?'

Blowing out a breath, he nodded. 'Deal.'

Inside the tavern, the lunchtime crowd was both noisy and merry, and Nina found herself grinning. It looked like a movie set—all stone and wood, and full of atmosphere. An impression that was immediately dispelled when a drunken man, all oily smiles and beery breath, leaned across to leer at her and offered to buy her a drink.

No, grazie.' With a shudder, she sidled away to order a white wine at the bar.

'Don't let Roberto put you off and give us a bad name,' a woman on her other side said in heavily accented English. 'He is…how do you say it? An eternal optimist. He lives in hope that one day someone will say yes.'

They both watched as he tried the same routine on the next woman who entered. Nina shook her head. 'One has to admire his tenacity, I guess.'

The other woman laughed. 'I'm Maria, and I don't recognise your accent. Where are you from?'

Blake strode into the bar ten minutes later and from her spot at Maria's table, Nina swore the entire crowd stilled to stare. The women sighed. The men puffed out their chests as if reminding themselves to be manly. It would've made her smile, except a deep hard longing gripped her. All she wanted to do was stride across the room, grab his arm, and drag him back to the yacht and have her wicked way with him.

Dear God, what was wrong with her? They'd spent the last five days doing exactly that. Surely the edge of her hunger should be blunted by now. But as a sultry brunette hip-swayed across to lean on the bar beside him, Nina had to fight the urge to immediately pull her hair into a ponytail.

Or to stride across and slip her arm through Blake's and stake her claim.

She shook herself. She and Blake might be fooling around at the moment, but it wasn't real. It was just a temporary fling—a clouds-in-your-coffee illusion with no basis in reality. It had no future.

Beside her Maria's brother Antonio explained the intricacies of making limoncello. She did her best to look interested. From the corner of her eye, she saw the smile Blake sent the sultry brunette and something in her heart cracked. How could he smile at someone else like that when—?

She froze. Panic surged in her throat. *No!* Oh, no, no, no!

She couldn't have gone and done the unthinkable. She *couldn't* have fallen in love with Blake? That would be emotional suicide! It could only lead to pain and heartache.

A *lot* of heartache.

Her eyes burned and her throat stretched into

a painful ache. It didn't matter if she pulled her hair into a thousand ponytails, falling in love with Blake was the one fate he could never rescue her from.

Her vision darkened at the edges and her temples throbbed, but slowly her chin came up. Not *couldn't*, but *wouldn't*. Blake would never risk his heart to save hers from breaking. He would never relinquish the lone-wolf mask he cherished so dearly.

Unless…

She bit her lip. Unless she could find a way to save him from himself.

Damn it! Nina didn't need rescuing. Not from men in danger of becoming too friendly nor from boredom. Or the inability to draw a stranger into conversation.

She sat at a table on the other side of the room with a group of people who all laughed at something she said. Yearning, hard and deep, gripped him. More than anything, he wanted to stride across and join them—to pull up a seat beside Nina and become a part of that relaxed, easy-going group.

He wasn't so good at relaxed and easy-going, though, was he? Maybe Nina was glad to have a break from him? The thought had his heart sinking like a giant-sized boulder.

The tall brunette who'd moved to stand beside

him, and now blocked his view of Nina and her party, said something to him when the barman ambled over in their direction, but his Italian was too limited to catch whatever it was she said. He gestured for her to order before him, angling his head around her, to find Nina staring at him. She glanced at the brunette and raised an eyebrow.

Hold on… She didn't think—

He would never fool around with another woman while he and Nina were…

Were what? Was there even a word to describe what they were doing, other than fooling around? They hadn't made any promises. Maybe she had romantic plans for one of the men at her table? Maybe she—

He shook the thought off. That wasn't what this bar challenge was about. It was about being comfortable in her own skin and confident enough to initiate conversation with a stranger.

A drink was set in front of him and he realised the brunette had ordered for him. He handed his credit card to the barman. Toasting the brunette, he tried not to shiver at the predatory expression in her eyes. When the barman handed him back his card, he excused himself with a nod.

Her face fell. In other circumstances he'd have taken the effort to make conversation with her, but he wasn't letting Nina think he was interested in another woman, not while they were *fooling around* together. Not for a single second. He wasn't giving her any reason to bring their arrangement to a screaming halt.

Nina's earlier words replayed themselves in his mind. *I like meeting new people...* The way she'd called him a liar when he'd said he did too.

Okay, so maybe he wasn't so good at putting himself out there. Maybe he'd taken the lone-wolf thing too far. But how hard could it be?

Taking a fortifying sip of his beer, he made towards a group of men. '*Scusi,* my Italian is terrible, *mi dispiace*—' *I'm sorry* '—but you gentlemen look as if you might be locals, and I wondered if I could ask your advice?'

They gave him wary, but encouraging nods.

'If I wanted to take a beautiful woman on a romantic dinner this evening, where in your opinion is the place to go?'

Faces lit up and hands rubbed together. Venues were debated and eventually a restaurant agreed upon, but the advice kept coming thick and fast. 'You want to take her on the perfect date, *sì*?'

'*Sì.*' Nina deserved the best.

He made notes on his phone as a full itinerary was created for him. Catching the barman's eye, he gestured for a round of drinks for his new friends. When he saw Nina's companions rise to leave, he excused himself with many thanks.

He met her halfway across the room. 'Have fun?'

She nodded. 'You?'

He frowned. He had.

'Why did you blow that gorgeous brunette off?'

The question had his stomach churning. Had she wanted him to hook up with another woman? 'Look, I know we're only fooling around, but I've no intention of looking at other women for as long as we are, okay?'

'Oh.' The air left her lungs on a soft rush, and something in her face softened too. He had to fight the urge not to drag her into his arms. 'Good to know,' she whispered.

She didn't trust him yet—not fully—but he'd win her trust back before they were done here in the Mediterranean. 'Also, she approached me, not the other way around. And as I didn't initiate anything, I figured it wasn't in the spirit of the challenge and shouldn't count.'

She frowned, her brows lowering over her eyes. 'Damn,' she murmured. 'Okay, hold on.' She lifted a finger, glanced around. 'I won't be a moment.'

Moving to the bar, she smiled at a woman and pointed to her feet. A lively discussion ensued and the play of expressions on Nina's face made him smile. He leaned against a tall table and finished his beer, soaking in the atmosphere, and the odd sense of feeling at home here—as if he belonged.

Nina moved back to him, huge smile on her face. 'Apparently Positano is known for its fabulous sandals. There are artisan shoemakers in the town who take your measurements and will make you a pair in half an hour. How cool is that?'

'Wanna go shopping?'

'Do you mind?'

'Not in the slightest.' Nina deserved every treat this trip could offer. 'Would you like to sample the delights of a local restaurant this evening? I have it on good authority that it shouldn't be missed.'

'Sounds great.'

Something an awful lot like happiness billowed in his chest. He'd made such a huge mistake in not returning to Callenbrook sooner—not just because in delaying it he'd freighted his return with too much pressure, but because he'd denied himself the pleasure of Nina's company for far too long. Sure, their telephone and video calls had kept them in touch, had been fun in their own way, but nothing could replace this face-to-face contact.

Or the full-body contact, a wicked voice whispered through him, drawing his skin tight. He'd miss that when this was all over.

Does it have to end?

Of course it did. He didn't do commitment or—

But neither of them was currently seeing anyone else. Maybe they could...

Could *what*? He frowned, but the question continued to plague him.

Pushing it away, he helped Nina search for a shoemaker. As she consulted with the artisan, he browsed the nearby shops and on the spur of the moment bought her a silk top in all the pretty colours of her garden.

She was waiting for him outside the artisan's workshop when he returned. He handed the bag to her. 'I saw this and thought of you.'

She blinked. And a slow smile spread across her face. She handed him a small parcel. 'Ditto.'

Grinning stupidly, he peeked inside to find a chic leather cardholder dyed a bright Mediterranean blue.

'To remind you of our trip. And because it's the same colour as your eyes,' she said.

'I love it.' He held her gaze. 'But I don't need anything to remember this trip by, Nina. This trip...*you*... It's the best time I've ever had.'

Her eyes widened and those delectable lips parted, and then her eyes filled. 'Don't you dare make me cry!'

He held up his hands. 'Wouldn't dream of it.' Though he found himself oddly hungry to hear her 'ditto' to his sentiment as well. *Loser.* 'What do you think?' He gestured to her bag she'd yet to open.

She gave a squeal of delight when she peeked inside. 'It's gorgeous! Oh, Blake, I love it! I'll wear it tonight.'

He beamed. And then she kissed him full on the lips in broad daylight in this extraordinary vertical city and he felt as if he were about to take off in flight.

She eased away. 'Now, what do you say to a gelato while we wait for my sandals? And then heading back to the yacht for a little afternoon siesta before our adventure tonight?'

The heated expression in her eyes told him that resting was the last thing on her mind. 'Excellent plan.'

They ate at a restaurant perched high on a clifftop with seats on a terrace that boasted one of the best views in all of Positano. Nina's awed expression had him feeling like a million bucks. She took her seat and rested her arms on the iron railing, rested her chin on her hands. 'Dear God, Blake, it doesn't matter what the food here tastes like, it's already the best restaurant in the world.'

'Best friend in the world,' he countered. She deserved it.

Her gaze flicked to him briefly before returning to the view.

'Best date in the world,' he added.

She straightened, mischief sparkling in her eyes. 'Best time you've ever had.'

Her grin was irresistible and he didn't try resisting it. 'For pity's sake, Nina, tell me this is better than line dancing at the community hall on a Saturday afternoon. You're killing me here.'

Her laugh bathed him in the same oranges and golds that stretched along the horizon. 'Only like a million times better. Blake, this trip… It's been extraordinary. I've had the most amazing time. And seeing you again…'

Her words trailed off and he nodded. 'I feel the same.'

She frowned for a moment, lips pursed. 'Do you?'

This woman had the most extraordinary heart and he hated that he'd hurt her. Reaching across, he took her hand. 'I swear to you that I won't ever let that same distance grow between us again.'

Warm caramel eyes searched his face. 'No?'

He crossed his heart with exaggerated care. 'You mean too much to me.'

'Good,' she said, almost to herself.

He released her hand. 'Now let's order and you can tell me if you've made any plans for the future yet.'

Luckily the food was every bit as good as the view. They ate seafood linguine and a salad lush with fragrant green leaves, juicy tomatoes and buffalo mozzarella while Nina outlined the degree she wanted to enrol in when she returned home. 'If my application is accepted, it will mean living in Melbourne during term time, which could be fun.'

He imagined her meeting new people, making new friends... He frowned. Meeting guys—or one guy in particular—and falling in love.

'What's wrong with my plan?'

He shook himself. 'Nothing! Sounds like fun. Was thinking, though, that there must be good degrees in environmental science in the UK as well.'

She folded her arms on the table in front of her.

'An international degree would be ludicrously expensive. Iris has left me very comfortably off, but I'm not rolling in money.'

'Ah, but I am.' And if Nina moved to the UK they could see each other all the time. It'd be brilliant.

She huffed out a laugh. 'You're ridiculously generous with your money, but no. This is something I'd like to do on my own.'

He couldn't blame her for that.

'And while you're my best friend...'

He could've wept in relief at that pronouncement. He'd come so close to messing it up and losing her friendship forever. To know she'd fully forgiven him was everything.

'All of my other friends live in Callenbrook and... I like the place.'

He wasn't sure he'd ever feel the same way, but he nodded to show he understood.

'And the other thing...'

He glanced up at the odd note in her voice.

She wrinkled her nose at him. 'If I moved to England I have a feeling I might be tempted to prolong this arrangement of ours and that's probably not a good idea.'

Actually, though...was it a bad idea?

He turned it over in his mind. You know what? He'd be totally and utterly on board with that. *Totally and utterly.* Before he could say as much, she changed the topic. 'I only have one more envelope to open from Iris.'

Only one? 'Amalfi?'

'Ravello.' She spooned lemon tiramisu into her mouth, pointed her spoon at him. For no reason at all, his mouth watered. 'This one's different from the others. I'm instructed to go to a particular spot and to only open the envelope once I'm there.'

'Wow. Okay.' What did Gran have planned for her? And, by extension, him, as he had no intention of leaving her to face any of these challenges on her own.

Best friends, that was what they were. And he'd stick by Nina through thick and thin, would face every challenge beside her. 'So...' He raised an eyebrow. 'Should we head to Amalfi tomorrow?' It would probably only take twenty minutes on the yacht. 'We can drive up to Ravello from there.'

'Yes, please.'

'Though maybe we won't leave too early. On the agenda this evening is dancing into the wee small hours at an exclusive club further along the beach from the marina—keeping our eyes peeled for the film stars and rock gods who frequent the place—followed by a light dessert at a little hole-in-the-wall joint that only the locals know about.'

'A second dessert!'

'We're on holiday, aren't we?'

She clasped her hands beneath her chin. Her eyes sparkled in the gathering darkness of the night, brighter than the lights of the boats in the harbour. 'If this place is so secret, how do you know about it?'

He stretched his legs out. 'Well, I was challenged to go into a bar and make conversation with strangers. I decided to ask said strangers where they'd take a beautiful woman on a date in Positano.'

Her mouth fell open.

'I told them she was special—that there was no one who meant more to me.'

Her eyes grew suspiciously bright.

'And I said I wanted to make memories that would last us both a lifetime and they gave me the inside intel.'

The gazes caught and held. Her eyes throbbed into his. 'I'm never going to forget,' she whispered.

'I'm never going to forget,' he whispered back.

It felt like a promise.

CHAPTER TEN

THIS TRIP, YOU... IT's the best time I've ever had.

There's no one who means more to me.

I wanted to make memories that will last a life-time.

As the car Blake had hired for them wound its way up to the hillside town of Ravello, Blake's words went around and around in Nina's mind—a litany of hope.

The way he'd looked at her last night, the way he'd made love with her, the things he'd said... Could it be that he'd fallen in love with her too and simply wasn't aware of it yet?

Could it be possible that she *hadn't* fallen in love with him, and that this was all a case of the romance of the trip going to her head? After the year she'd had, that'd be understandable, right?

But...

After a truly memorable night of dancing and spotting famous faces, and eating delicious cannoli at a ridiculous time in the morning, the two of them had stumbled back to the yacht in a haze of passion to make love with an intensity that had stretched each moment out into a celebration of joy and... *Love*.

That was what it had felt like and none of it was due to the exotic beauty of the Mediterranean or a result of her grief. It was due to Blake.

His quiet strength, his endless generosity, his determined persistence in winning back her friendship. Her joy in seeing him eventually relax and unwind and find joy again—it had set something free inside her. She'd fallen in love with *him*. The Mediterranean setting was just an added bonus.

Seeing him again after so long, even when she'd been angry with him, had felt like a piece of her clicking back into place—as if she hadn't been whole without him. Like a jigsaw puzzle with a piece missing.

Her mouth dried. If she wasn't whole without him... Her hands clenched, her fingernails digging into her palms. Telling him how she felt had the potential to rain disaster down on their heads. If he didn't feel the same way she could ruin everything—their friendship, his peace of mind and her own.

Things inside her shrank and shrivelled. If he didn't feel the same way, she might never see him again and surely that would be the worst outcome of all. It'd be better to keep all of this to herself. At least she'd still have his friendship. At least she'd get to see him at Christmas, have multiple video calls with him throughout the year.

She swallowed. Maybe, eventually, what she felt for him would fade.

Ha! That thinking was as falsely optimistic as drunken Roberto in yesterday's lunchtime bar hoping for a date. *Not* going to happen.

Maybe when Blake returned home to London he'd discover how much he missed her and realise he'd fallen in love with her?

And pigs might fly.

She recalled the way they'd made love the previous night and her heart surged against the walls of her chest, refusing to give up hope. It *had* to be possible.

'You're very quiet,' Blake said beside her, shrewd eyes raking her face. 'Tired?'

No closer to sorting out the best course of action to take where she and Blake were concerned, she pushed it to the back of her mind. She had time to puzzle it out. After Amalfi they were heading to Corfu for a few days. *There's time.* 'A little.' She smiled and shrugged. 'Aren't you?'

Reaching out, he took her hand and threaded his fingers through hers. 'Yep, but it was worth it.' Those shrewd eyes travelled over her face again. 'Are you nervous about whatever Gran is going to say to you in her letter?'

She rubbed her other hand over her chest to ease the sudden ache that stretched across her heart. 'A little. I mean to embrace whatever challenge she's set for me, because…'

'Because?'

'I trust her. She hasn't led me astray—not once—even though I've found some of her challenges hard, like the parasailing and the bikini.'

'And the skinny-dipping.'

His lips curved and she couldn't help but laugh. 'Each of those things has pushed me out of my comfort zone and made me braver. All of it has made me feel better about whatever the future might hold.'

Even if that future doesn't contain Blake?

Stop it! She refused to even contemplate that at the moment. Shaking it off, she managed a wobbly smile. 'But whatever is in the final envelope, they'll be her last words to me and…'

His hand tightened about hers. 'You don't want it to come to an end.'

For as long as she'd had those sealed envelopes, all waiting to be opened, she'd felt as though Iris were with her, almost as if she were on this trip with them. Once she opened the final letter, that illusion would dissolve.

'It's not the end, Nina. You'll always carry her in your heart. *Always.*'

The truth of that had her spine straightening. Blake was right. She would.

It seemed serendipitous as at that exact moment they drove into the township of Ravello. They didn't linger to admire the quaint cobbled streets or the pretty buildings or the historic timeless essence of the town, but made directly for Villa Rufolo and the famous view of the Amalfi Coast from its terrace. It was feted as one of the most beautiful views in the world.

With the high season over, they were lucky enough to find themselves alone on the terrace. Nina might still feel a little nervous of heights, but she couldn't prevent her feet from taking her to the very edge of the terrace to stare out at the incredible view. In fact, if the railing hadn't been there she might've stepped right into it.

Blake slipped an arm around her shoulders and she leaned into him. 'Now that's something,' he breathed.

All she could do was nod. Below them the deep blue of the water stretched out to the horizon—the air so crisp and clear it made everything *sparkle*. The collection of white buildings below and the curve of the white pebbled beach provided a perfect foil and contrast for all of that blue. And with no breeze ruffling the water and, therefore, no white caps, the view looked utterly serene. The silhouette of a pine tree, its darkness and the beauty of its symmetry, added a note of unexpected perfection to the already stunning scene.

'Granny Day would've loved this.'

'She'd have sat here and fixed it in her mind—

memorising every single detail so she could take this view home with her.'

She gave a soft laugh in recognition because that was exactly what Iris would've done. 'If it wasn't for her, we'd probably have never seen this.'

'And that would have been a loss.'

They stared at the view for a long time. Eventually, silently, Nina moved to a stone bench and pulled out Iris's final envelope from her pocket. Caressing the familiar writing, she slid her finger beneath the sealed flap and drew out a single sheet of paper.

Do you know what a privilege it has been to have you in my life, Nina? I count myself the most fortunate of women.

The page blurred. Blinking back tears, Nina read on.

She read to the end and then stared unseeingly at the view, the letter clasped in her hand—her heart throbbing and her mind churning.

She started when a soft hand brushed the hair back from her face. 'You okay?'

Lifting her hands to her cheeks, she found them wet. He handed her an immaculate white cotton handkerchief. She handed him the letter.

He read it out aloud, his voice warm and reverent.

'Of course my final challenge is the hardest. It was always going to be. It's hard because it's a lifelong challenge. It's what all of the other challenges have been leading you towards. And it is merely this...

'Nina, I ask you to not hold yourself back. I want you to live your life to the full, and you can only do that if you open your heart to embrace all that life has to offer. We are here on this earth for such a short time, put yourself out there and take risks. It's not the times we make fools of ourselves that we live to regret, it's the risks we didn't take, the times we kept our hearts and our egos safe behind our walls, that will come back to haunt you. Don't put off until some indeterminate date in the future the things you ache to do. Instead, if you can, do them as soon as possible.

'There will be times when this open-hearted approach to life leaves you vulnerable, leaves you open to hurt and heartache, but I promise you will recover from both of those things, although it might take some time. Nina, you're intelligent and capable and you once had big dreams. Dreams you put on hold because of your love for two older women—your mother

and me. Love is never a bad choice, but it's time now to dust off your dreams and to follow them wherever they may lead you. So my final challenge to you, my darling girl, is to live fearlessly, to live in a way that makes you proud of yourself every single day.'

Blake halted as he came to the end. It was signed, *your ever-loving Iris, your Granny Day, the grandmother of your heart.* The words were burned on her heart.

As Blake had read the letter out, Nina had moved back to stand at the railing, wanting to reach out and grab some of that view's serenity, some of its peace, and push it inside her throbbing chest.

Open your heart to embrace all that life has to offer.

Live fearlessly.

It's the risks we don't take that haunt us.

Iris's words rolled through her mind, gaining momentum, urging her to take the biggest risk of her life. Blood thundered in her ears, drowning out the song of a nearby warbler.

Blake moved to stand beside her, folded the single sheet of paper and handed it back to her. 'It's a hell of a letter, Nina.'

She slid it back into its envelope and pressed it to her heart for a moment before sliding it back into her pocket. 'Could you live your life like that, Blake?'

He shook his head. 'I don't think so.'

She half turned to him and he shrugged. 'Sometimes there are very good reasons for being cautious and protecting yourself.'

'I don't think she's saying be reckless or foolhardy, or that there's never a need for caution.'

'I expect you're right.'

There was something in his voice, though. 'But?'

He grimaced, shrugged. 'There's no doubting that my grandmother was a wise woman...'

Absolutely no doubt.

'But I can't help feeling her advice in that letter...' He rolled his shoulders. 'It seems naïve, is all.'

Opposition immediately rose inside her. In her letter Iris had boiled life down to its simplest form, but Blake always had to make things complicated. He always searched for the flaws and the weaknesses and the risks involved. And in doing that, he so often prevented himself from living in the moment.

'I think both our lives could be improved if we followed Iris's advice.' One sceptical eyebrow rose and she tapped a finger against his chest. 'You'd have *never* gone skinny-dipping if you hadn't shrugged off your fear and decided to take a risk. And that was an unforgettable experience.'

He straightened. 'I wasn't *scared*.'

'You were scared of stepping outside conventions, scared that people might hear about the exploit, and you were worried about being arrested.'

'The latter was a legitimate concern!'

'It was *never* going to happen.'

Blowing out a breath, he shook his head. 'There's nothing wrong with being cautious.'

'Except you're so often trading joy for it, Blake, and that seems too high a price to pay.'

'It's not like I'm *never* relaxed and happy.' He stared at her for a long moment. 'Surely this trip has proven that?'

She chewed on her bottom lip. 'It's not wholehearted, though,' she said slowly.

His gaze narrowed, and those two halves of her immediately went to war. *Don't rock the boat. Don't ruin the most important friendship of your life.*

It's the risks we don't take that haunt us.

Far below the church bell sounded, and very slowly Nina straightened. 'The thing is, Blake, I still think you live your life crippled by fear.'

His head rocked back, and she quickly shook hers. 'I'm not talking about your panic attacks. The fact you've dealt with those and overcome them—or have learned how to manage them— proves you've the strength and the courage to live life fearlessly. If you choose to.'

Slamming both hands to his hips, he half glared at her. 'How can you both insult and compliment me in almost the same breath?'

Her hands went to her hips then too. 'Because I want you to be happy. Fully and wholly and fearlessly happy. Not just half happy.'

'I *am* happy!'

'And yet in swearing to never fall in love—in keeping your heart safe—you're denying yourself the promise of a very special and very real form of happiness.' It made her want to scream in frustration.

His face hardened. '*That's* a risk I'm prepared to make. There are other forms of happiness, other ways to be happy.'

With a frustrated slash of her hand, she swung away. 'Of course there are, but why deny yourself any of them? *That's* what's so senseless.'

'You know my reasons, Nina,' he said quietly.

She turned back, her heart thud-thud-thudding. 'What? That whole lone-wolf thing? Is that really so precious to you?' Did he seriously want to walk alone his entire life? 'This is because of your mother, isn't it? Because she manipulated you and you won't ever give anyone that power over you again. You live in fear of becoming your father.'

Closing his eyes, he bent at the waist to rest his hands on his knees. She sensed he was counting his breaths, and her hands twisted together. She didn't want to trigger a panic attack. She didn't want to be the cause of so much stress.

Closing her eyes too, she counted to three. How could she convince him to open up his heart? 'Your grandmother, my mother and I always treated you with thoughtfulness and respect. We never betrayed your trust or let you down. Why isn't *our* influence and *our* example the one you're choosing to follow rather than your mother's?' Her words were a cry on the air, a plea. For him to choose love and connection and happiness.

Slowly he straightened, those extraordinary eyes meeting hers. 'There's no denying what my parents did has cast a shadow over my life, but you're wrong to think they still have that kind of hold on me. Those shadows aren't so dark any more.' His hands clenched and unclenched. 'I've made progress in these last few months, Nina. I'm mostly in control of my panic attacks. I was able to return to Callenbrook.' He pulled in a breath. 'I've been able to fix our friendship.'

Could he not see how much more their friendship could be, though?

His lips twisted into a half-smile. 'What's more, miracles of miracles, I've become less stuffy and less boring, and that's due to you. I'm letting fun and creativity back into my life. And I mean to keep implementing improvements once I'm home.'

She was glad to hear it. And glad too that he could recognise the progress he'd made. 'So what's holding you back from letting love into your life as well?'

'My best way of coping long term is as a lone wolf, Nina, you have to see that.' He started to pace. 'I don't want to pull anyone else into my issues. I've come so far and I'm in a stable place. In what universe would I risk destabilising that?' He swung back with a hard shake of his head. 'I'd have to be a fool.'

Her jaw dropped.

He held a hand up before she could speak. 'I know what you're going to say, but think about it. Whatever else you want to say about love, you also have to admit that it's intense and chaotic and volatile. That is *not* for me.'

She stared at him.

He rolled his shoulders. 'Stop looking at me like that.'

Her heart thundered in her ears. 'You're saying you'd rather keep your life calm and on an even keel than take a risk on something that could add more fun and creativity to your life—and so much *joy*. That's your stuffy, risk-averse side talking, Blake. You're only seeing potential negatives and not the positives. You think of love as something that could mess with your peace of mind—something that has the potential not just to rock your boat but to overturn it—but what if love is like parasailing? What if it's freedom and floating and a safe harbour?'

His face tightened. 'What if it's a cold plunge in the ocean?'

'What if it brings more that's good to your life than bad?'

His eyes flashed. 'What if it's simply not a risk I'm prepared to take?' Planting his feet, he folded his arms. 'Why the hell does this matter so much to you anyway?'

'Because I love you, Blake!' She hadn't meant to blurt the words out so baldly, but they'd been pressing against her throat with increasing fierceness until she couldn't hold them back. 'And I'm not talking about the love friends have for one another.' She pointed an unsteady finger at him. 'I'm *in* love with you.'

The colour drained from his face. He took a step back...shook his head.

She wasn't sure how his body managed it, but it was as if it had sagged and turned to steel at the same time. And his horror was like a scythe, cutting her soul adrift from the rest of her body and turning her to ice. She imagined jagged icicles radiating outwards from her heart, cutting a path through her chest, stabbing and piercing.

'You *can't* have.' He choked out the denial. His neck had gone stiff, so had his shoulders. The muscles in his forearms strained—as if they were trying to hold back disaster.

The intensity of his opposition beat and buffeted her. Her lungs cramped. Her throat stretched into a painful ache. It took a force of will to remain standing.

What did you expect? Had you really thought

he'd sweep you up in his arms and tell you he loved you too?

Maybe not. But with all of herself she'd hoped he would.

From somewhere she found the strength to swallow. His reaction was the stuff of nightmares, but it was also exactly what half of her had expected. And at least now she knew.

And there's comfort in that?

Digging deep, she shoved that thought away to seize her composure and wrap it around her like a blanket. She would *not* cry in front of him. She could at least spare him that.

Hitching up her chin, she shrugged. 'I didn't mean to. And if I could change it I would. But I can't.'

The world had stopped turning. That was what it felt like. The natural world had stopped operating the way it ought to. Blake opened his mouth, but couldn't force anything past the hot lump of lava in his throat.

'That's why this matters so much to me, Blake.' Nina's lips twisted. 'Maybe now you'll understand why I'm arguing for you to open up your heart.'

Her words burned through him like acid, leaving him scalded and charred.

She shrugged. 'I love you.'

She had to stop saying that!

His vision darkened, his chest cramped and his

breathing grew rapid. It took all his strength to focus on slowing his breaths. Staring at the ground, he found three separate objects and focused on them—a pretty pink pebble, a butterfly and a tiny flower that looked like a daisy. He counted in threes backwards from forty. A little calmer, he glanced across to where she stood.

She stared out at the view, that lovely lower lip of hers caught between her teeth, and the light in those beautiful eyes dim and unseeing. He wanted to throw his head back and howl. She *loved* him. With every atom of himself, he wanted that to *not* be true. She meant so much to him—she was the most important person in his life—but to tell her that would give her the wrong impression. He couldn't give her what she needed. 'Nina…'

Her name emerged as a croak—his throat a pitiful, painful, stretched thing—and she had the temerity to glance back at him and roll her eyes. 'God, Blake, don't say anything. *Please*. Believe me, I can see exactly how you feel. Don't make it worse.'

It *couldn't* get any worse.

'I never expected you to return my feelings.' She gave a suspiciously casual shrug. 'Not really.'

'Then why tell me?' Why had she made herself so vulnerable? She had to know he couldn't give her what she wanted. *Nobody* knew him as well as she did.

She raised an eyebrow. 'You think I should've kept it to myself and suffered in silence?'

Damn it. *No.* He didn't want her suffering at all.

She touched a hand to her pocket where Gran's letter rested. 'I told you because of what Iris said about living fearlessly. And when all's said and done, I think I'd rather know the truth.'

'I'm sorry I can't give you what you want.' It felt as if invisible walls were closing around him, pressing the air from his body. It would've been better for her if he'd never returned to Callenbrook.

She gave another of those suspiciously casual shrugs. He wanted to shout at her to stop doing that. Which didn't make any sense. She was simply trying to make the best of a bad situation.

'People survive broken hearts, Blake. They do it all the time. Iris survived when your grandad died; Mum survived my father's feet of clay. And I'll survive this.' Her eyes flashed. 'I'm not weak like my father *or* yours.'

He nodded. 'I know.'

'And *you're* not weak like your father either.'

Her words speared into the secret depths of the sorest part of his heart. At the moment, he sure as hell didn't feel strong. She'd moved further and further away from him as she'd clocked his reaction to her *news*, but she moved closer now, pushing into his personal space until all he could feel was her heat and all he could smell was the scent of amber and jasmine. And all he could think about was her.

'And here's something else for you to stick in your pipe and smoke on.'

It was an old expression of Gran's and almost made him smile. Maybe he would have if he'd not been concentrating so fiercely on fighting the urge to claim her lips with his. To kiss her now would be unforgivable. She might know him better than anyone, but he knew her too. He couldn't—*wouldn't*—give her false hope.

'I think you're half in love with me too, Blake, and just too afraid to admit it.'

It took a moment for her words to collide with his grey matter. When they did he took an involuntary step backwards.

A hand reached out and squeezed the air from his body. She *had* to be wrong. He wasn't falling in love with anyone. He was finally in a stable place and he wasn't letting anything mess with that. All he wanted was to consolidate—to remain in London, see his therapist if and when he needed to, and to continue to slowly and quietly improve his life. To shore it up against the possibility of future mayhem and trauma.

He'd never been interested in letting something as wild and unpredictable as love into his life and he was even less interested after wrestling with his panic attacks. He craved a quiet life of quiet accomplishment, but it wouldn't be a life devoid of fun. Not any more. And once in a blue moon he'd push himself outside his comfort zone because it'd be good for him. But he wanted nothing to do with an emotion like love. Its turbulence and instability had the potential to derail his life. And him.

His hands clenched. He'd fought too hard to get to where he was, to get his panic attacks mostly under control. He wasn't regressing, relapsing or letting his guard down now.

'And just so you know…'

He wanted to close his ears against the sound of Nina's voice. He didn't know when it had happened, but her voice had started to sound like a siren's song.

'When I refer to love, I'm not confusing it with sex.' She paced back to the railing. 'Mind you, the sex has been off-the-charts spectacular.'

Don't think about the sex! There'd be no more of that now, and a chasm opened up inside him.

'Right, so here's the deal, Blake. I'm giving you until Corfu to think about everything I've said and come to your senses.'

Her words had him stiffening. Was she *threatening* him? 'And if I haven't changed my mind by then?'

She folded her arms and stuck out one hip. '*You're* the best time I ever had. There's *no one* who means more to me. I want to make memories that will last us a *lifetime*.'

He flinched as she tossed his words back at him. He hadn't meant them like *that*.

'What about the way you're so protective of me?'

That was natural!

'And how you get grumpy-jealous if you think I'm having "fun" with some other guy.'

That wasn't jealousy. He ground his teeth together. *It wasn't.*

'And there's the way you want me to relocate to the UK.'

Because she was his friend—his *best* friend—nothing more. It was only natural to want to see more of her.

'And how much time and energy you expend making sure I'm having fun—the dates you planned.'

That was just good manners; him being a good host.

'If I'm wrong…'

She shrugged, but just for a moment he glimpsed the shadows in her eyes—shadows he'd caused unknowingly—and he wanted to throw his head back and howl.

'Then nothing, I suppose. Nothing happens. I'll fly back to Australia. You'll fly back to London. We get on with our lives.'

Of course she wasn't threatening him. But like an arrow finding the bullseye, he realised in that moment that she needed to protect herself too. His lungs laboured like billows, but rather than pumping air through his body they pumped fear. What about his and Nina's friendship? What about the future? What about...?

'And Christmas?' he choked out.

Shadowed eyes met his. 'I'm not thinking beyond Corfu at the moment. Come on, it's time to head back to the yacht.'

The journey to Corfu was a nightmare. Mealtimes were stilted and awkward. He spent most of his time in the library-cum-office, staring at the walls. At one point he ventured out to the hot tub, hoping the heated jets of water would work out the knots in his back and shoulders.

Nina appeared a short time later, obviously with the same intention. The moment she saw him, she veered away, but he immediately leaped out of the water. 'It's all yours. I'm done. In danger of turning into a prune if I stay in any longer,' he babbled.

She turned back and her gaze settled for a long moment on his wet chest—her gaze darkening and her throat bobbing as she swallowed. A few days ago she'd have joined him and—

He had to fight the urge to stalk across and kiss her, to carry her down to her cabin and make love with her until neither one of them could think straight. But if he did that he'd be making a promise—a forever kind of promise he had no hope of keeping. He couldn't hurt her like that.

Loss nearly buckled his knees when he walked away.

He agonised over what to say to her when they reached Corfu. Searched for the right words that would let her down easily. Did such words exist? He didn't want to hurt her—he'd sacrifice a limb not to. But he couldn't give her what she wanted.

When they reached Corfu harbour he remained in his room later than usual, like a coward. Aurelia had tapped on his door to check if he'd like her to clean his cabin. He'd told her not to bother, but had asked after Nina. She'd apparently set off to explore the island an hour earlier.

Without him?

You've no right to feel hurt or wounded or—

He'd never felt more confused in his life. Stalking up on deck, he stared at the sandstone buildings of Corfu, at its two Venetian fortresses, at all of the people bustling along the waterfront, and threw himself down onto a sun lounger. Why did Nina have to go and do something stupid like fall in love with him anyway? She *knew* him. She *knew* his stance on relationships and commitment. She'd had to know it'd end in tears.

Damn it all to hell! They should never have given into their attraction. She'd been right when she'd said sex complicated everything.

But she'd also said their friendship would survive it. He clung to that promise. Come Christmas, hopefully they'd be able to laugh about this.

He mooched about on the yacht all day, restless and aimless. At some point he found his way back to the sun lounger and threw himself down on it. The warm air conspiring with a poor night's sleep had him closing his eyes.

He must've dozed off. He slowly came awake as someone gently nudged his foot and a couple of drops of water splashed his toes. He opened his eyes to find Nina standing at the bottom of the sun lounger, her sunglasses and hat in place, making it hard to decipher her expression, but she held a beer in one hand and a glass of white wine in the other. It was the condensation from the bottle of beer that had dripped on him.

She silently handed him the beer—before settling into the other sun lounger. The sun had started to set, but the air was warm even as the shadows lengthened. 'So what's your verdict?'

She asked her question at the exact moment he took his first sip of beer and he nearly choked. 'You did that on purpose!'

She shrugged, her lips twitching. 'Maybe.'

He couldn't help but grin. He'd missed this—the fun and the teasing. He'd missed *her*. 'What? No small talk first?' Couldn't they have a little more camaraderie, a little more banter and friendship before he broke her heart? 'What was Corfu like?'

She gestured out in front of them. 'It's right there, Blake. Go and experience it for yourself.'

He hadn't had the energy today. He hadn't had the heart. Maybe tomorrow.

She met his gaze. 'And I really don't see the point in beating about the bush, do you?'

Yes! Just for a moment he wanted to luxuriate in her company, for them to be easy with one another. He wanted to delay what was coming—a temporary separation while she worked through her hurt feelings. Hurt he wished he could spare her.

'So, answer the question, Blake. Can you see any future for us romantically?'

Silently he swore. He pulled in a breath, his hands clenching so hard around his bottle of beer he was amazed it didn't crack. 'I'm sorry, Nina, but I can't. No.'

She didn't look surprised, but something tightened in her face all the same. 'You really think we'd play out the same scenario as your mother and father?'

He recalled the utter shock of discovering that his mother had used him—the sense of betrayal. He remembered the cruel smile that had played around Mr Hutchinson's mouth as those five boys had punched and kicked Blake. He'd trusted both of them, had admired them both, and they'd betrayed him in the worst way possible. That buried trauma had nearly crippled him earlier in the year.

He trusted Nina too, but he was never giving her

the chance to betray him like that. If she betrayed him, he wasn't sure he'd survive it.

'Look, Nina, this isn't about you. It's about me. I'm just not prepared to risk it.'

'Even if you break your own heart in the process?'

He set his beer down. 'Gran said broken hearts mend. You believe that too.'

'I have to believe it,' she said with a bluntness that made him flinch.

'Then if that's what I'm doing—breaking my own heart—I guess I'll survive it as well.' It would be better than the pain of another betrayal, of trying to find a way to pick up the pieces again and go on. Of having to try and gather the shreds of himself back together in the midst of panic attacks that hit without warning.

In one lithe movement, she stood. He did too, swearing when he knocked over his beer. Throwing a nearby towel over the spill, he swung back. 'I'll still come to Callenbrook for Christmas.' He meant to say it like a statement—a non-negotiable fact—but it emerged more as a question—a panicked question.

'Let's skip Christmas this year,' Nina said, not meeting his eyes.

What the hell…? 'You said our friendship would survive us making love!'

For a moment she looked completely and utterly lost. His hands clenched and unclenched. He wanted to haul her into his arms and hug her.

'I thought it would.' Her eyes suddenly flashed. 'But I'm not omniscient so maybe I was wrong!'

A vice tightened about his chest. She couldn't be wrong. *She couldn't be wrong.*

She strode away from him then and that was when he saw the packed suitcase sitting just inside the door. His heart pounded up into his throat. 'What are you doing?'

For the briefest of moments her eyes met his. 'I'm going home, Blake. We did what we came here to do. It's time to go home.'

Seizing her suitcase, she walked down the short gangway to the dock below and strode into the gathering dusk and he'd never felt more alone in his life. He had to fix this. He couldn't lose Nina—not completely.

The thought was unthinkable. Unbearable.

CHAPTER ELEVEN

IT TOOK ALL of Blake's strength—every single morsel of it—to not race after Nina and beg her to come back to the yacht.

Beg her to come back to him.

He couldn't do that when he couldn't give her what she wanted—what she *needed*. The fact that he couldn't ate him alive.

He couldn't go after her, but he couldn't remain like some caged animal on the yacht either. Instead he vaulted down to the pier and paced the harbour and all of its surrounding streets, vaguely aware of magnificent date palms, the intoxicating scent of night jasmine, grand sandstone buildings, and the shrill cries of the sea birds mingling with the laughter of the holidaymakers spilling onto the streets from the restaurants and bars as the afternoon deepened to evening.

A couple of days ago he and Nina had been one of their number—holidaymakers having the time of their lives in Positano. With all of himself, he wished they could be doing that again in this equally extraordinary place. Without Nina, though, this place didn't feel extraordinary. It felt dull and grey and joyless.

He forced himself to look around, to really look. Corfu Town wasn't dull or grey. It was golden sandstone, whitewashed walls, and colourful flowers in overflowing pots, lush shrubs, and twinkling lights. It was heaven on earth.

It was *he* who was dull and grey and joyless—all of him, inside and out. He halted. This was like that first day in Cannes when Nina had ventured out without him—actively avoiding him. Only a hundred times worse because now she was gone. He had no hope of seeing her later this evening or tomorrow. No hope that he could make things right.

When parasailing with her in Nice, he'd finally glimpsed the magic of the French Riviera—why everyone waxed so lyrical about it. Monte Carlo with Nina had cemented in his mind the region's magic and glamour. And Portofino hadn't just revealed all that was good and bright about the Mediterranean, it had made him... He shook his head. It had made him feel alive again.

Which begged the question, when had he stopped living? When he was fifteen and three people he'd loved and admired—his mother, his father and Mr Hutchinson—had betrayed him?

He hadn't stopped living, but he *had* surrounded himself with prickly walls and kept people at arm's length. He'd worked hard, had made a lot of money, and he was proud of all he'd achieved, but he could count the number of friends he had on one hand. And even with them he maintained a certain distance, an aloofness. As for fun... Somewhere along the way he'd seemed to have banished it from his life. *Why?*

Because to have fun, one needed to embrace life wholeheartedly. In the way Gran in her last letter had urged Nina to live her life.

In Portofino, he'd let his barriers down at Nina's urging and had discovered a whole new world. And now that world was gone. Vanished as if by a click of magic fingers.

Thrusting out his jaw, he dragged in a breath and forced his feet forward again. He was overreacting, that was what he was doing. Meeting up with Nina again had been intense, a roller-coaster ride. Now it was time for life to get back to normal. And for him to remember what was important—that his life was stable and balanced and strong. It had only become that way through sheer hard work. He wasn't endangering the peace he'd worked so hard to achieve.

And yet he spent the following day once again tramping the streets of Corfu, not taking in the sights, not interested in the history of the place, not seeing the beauty. The day was the same grey and joyless canvas it had been the previous day. Why did Nina leave as she had? Why did she have to go and do something as stupid as fall in love with him? Throwing himself down to a bench, he rested his elbows on his knees and stared unseeingly at the ground. Everything felt wrong. And he was powerless to make it right.

'It is trouble of the heart, I think.'

He glanced to the side to find an older man on the bench beside him. He straightened, realising he'd slammed himself down beside the older man without so much as a by your leave. 'I'm sorry. I think I have disturbed you and—'

'No, no.'

Blake dragged a hand down his face. He needed to get out of his own head and pay attention to his surroundings. He had no right to inflict his misery on others. He gestured around, though a smile was beyond him. 'You are a local? You live here in Corfu?'

'Yes.'

He forced himself to be polite. 'It is a beautiful place.'

The other man stared at him for a long moment. 'I am an old man. I have lived, and seen much. But the expression on your face, the way your shoulders droop, tells me that you are not interested in the scenery, no.' He tapped his chest. 'You are afflicted with a soreness, a trouble of the heart.'

Was it that obvious? Blowing out a breath, Blake stared at the harbour. 'Your English is very good.'

'I worked in America for a couple of years when I was a younger man. When I returned home, I left my heart there.' He nodded. 'Yes, there are hurts that pierce deeper than others, hurts that stay with us.'

Like betrayal and the breaking of trust.

The older man pressed a hand to his chest. 'Tell me about your girl.'

The old Blake would've thanked him politely, risen and walked away. But the old Blake had lost Nina. Old Blake was a fool. 'She's not my girl. She *was* my best friend, though.'

The older man's eyes brightened. 'When friendship evolves into love, it is a thing of beauty.'

If one was interested in making a commitment, perhaps. He considered the wild ride of the last few weeks and managed a smile. 'I hadn't seen her face to face in a long time and when I did...' He shrugged. 'She'd become so beautiful.'

The old man laughed and clapped. 'Your boy's regard had become a man's regard. But, my son, this is the best way. You learn a whole new side to one another.'

A familiar heat rose through him when he recalled exactly what learning about that whole new side of Nina had involved.

'And you already know the... I do not know the way to say it in English. The soul, the quality, of each other's hearts.'

The soul of each other's hearts... He found himself smiling at that. 'Nina has the best heart in the world.'

The old man spread his hands. 'Then what is the complication? Does she not feel the same way?'

'*I* am the complication. I *don't* want to fall in love.'

It's too late for that, buddy.

The revelation didn't even surprise him. But knowing without a doubt that he loved Nina the way she wanted him to love her made it that much harder to not go after her.

The old man stared. 'You have been betrayed before, I think.'

He said nothing.

'And you are afraid your friend who you now love will betray you too.' He nodded and sighed. 'Our friends often have more power to hurt us than our lovers do.'

Blake's heart throbbed. He'd hurt Nina badly earlier in the year and yet she'd forgiven him. And now he'd hurt her again. He prayed to God she was okay.

'Has she ever betrayed you as a friend?'

Of course not.

The older man nodded as if reading the answer in Blake's face. 'Then here is a lesson learned from an old man. If you do not let love into your life, it is not just that you turn your back on light and joy, you embrace their opposites. Your life will become cold and hard. Unrelenting. Dull. And not just your life, but eventually you yourself too.'

What the hell…? He stared, aghast.

'It is not a course I recommend.'

Hell, no. He didn't want to become that person.

'If she has never betrayed you as a friend…'

But what if she did now or some time in the future? How would he survive it?

'If the quality of her heart—a heart you know and tell me it is the best heart in the whole world—is not in question…'

His mouth dried. The quality of Nina's heart…?

No. The quality of Nina's heart wasn't in question. *His* was.

That particular organ started to pound. *Hard.* He swallowed and tried to make his mind work. 'Nina isn't like my mother,' he said slowly. 'She doesn't take things away from people or make life less. She gives. She gives all of herself. She adds *richness* to everything.'

The old man eyed him steadily.

If anyone was in danger of being manipulated, it was Nina, not him. And he would *never* manipulate her. The thought of trying to manipulate anyone was abhorrent to him. It was a terrible thing to do. But to manipulate Nina, to break trust with her…

He pressed a hand to his brow, his mind racing. Nina wasn't like his father either. And he *wasn't* like his mother.

Nina might be generous and easy-going, but she also had a strong moral code. He might be able to talk her into gambling away a ridiculous amount of money for one night in Monte Carlo, but he'd never succeed in getting her to risk everything that Gran had left her.

His caged heart pounded against the walls of his chest. She might be able to talk him into skinny-dipping from their yacht in the middle of the night, but it wouldn't occur to her to do such a thing on a public beach. And even if it did, he'd refuse to take part. And she *wouldn't* hold that against him.

All of this time he'd considered love something that would steal his strength, steal his peace of mind and emotional stability, and overturn his life. But love—real love—didn't steal. It gave. It gave unstintingly. Nina was right. Love gave you the strength to weather the storms that came into your life. *It* wasn't the storm.

Nina had tried to tell him that but he hadn't listened.

'I think perhaps you have found a solution, *nai.*'

The older man beamed at him. Blake stared back, the coldness and darkness inside him receding. 'I think perhaps you're right.'

He leaped to his feet and prayed to God he hadn't left it too late. 'What did you do?' The older man blinked and Blake had to stifle a surge of uncharacteristic impatience. 'The girl in America who you loved?'

The older man's face cleared. 'I went back for her and asked her to marry me. Best thing I ever did. We were married and came here to live, had two sons. We had a long and happy life together.'

Had?

As if reading the question in Blake's eyes, the other man shook his head. 'She is no longer with us, sadly, but the memories keep me warm at night. I cherish them.'

Blake held out his hand. 'Thank you.'

The older man shook it. 'Good luck and God-speed.'

Nina attacked the second garden bed with exactly the same vigour as she had the first. She had no intention of letting the apathy of a broken heart get the better of her.

Ten minutes later, she dropped down to sit on the edge of the garden bed—a thick wooden sleeper—her trowel dangling uselessly in her fingers and the scent of the earth rising up around her. God, what was the point of it all?

Fresh fruit and vegetables.

Pretty flowers for the bees.

Those things had been important to her once.

They will be again.

That voice sounded suspiciously like Iris's. She glanced up at the sky. *Hurt and heartache, but I promise you'll recover from both those things.* 'Yeah, but you didn't tell me how long it would take,' she grumbled.

How long would she feel like this? As though

nothing mattered. As if the world were coming to an end. As if there'd never be joy or happiness or laughter in her life again. She just wanted to close her eyes and sleep for a hundred years. Whenever she closed her eyes, though, Blake's face appeared in her mind's eye and sleep evaded her.

It had taken an epic thirty-six hours to get home to Callenbrook. The logical part of her brain told her jet lag was playing havoc with her moods. A more knowing, deeper part of her brain told her heartbreak sucked ferociously and it'd be a while yet before the metaphorical sun came out again.

In the meantime all she could do was plant one foot in front of the other and do what needed doing, and hope that eventually she'd find pleasure in the things she once had. Like gardening. Her lips twisted. Like line dancing on a Saturday afternoon at the community hall.

She slumped—shoulders, spine and all. If she'd been made of wax, she'd have melted to a puddle on the ground. Not good for the plants and the soil or the birds and the bees. Not good for her either.

Annoyingly, she found herself constantly worried about Blake too. She knew he'd be gutted. She wanted to ring him and tell him she was okay, but she didn't *feel* okay and she knew he'd hear that in her voice. She knew what their friendship meant to him, because it had meant the same to her— and she wanted to ring and apologise that she'd wrecked it all by falling in love with him.

She wanted to weep that he'd shut love so completely and utterly out of his life. He'd been betrayed so badly by the people he'd looked up to, the people who should've looked after him. Maybe it was unfair of her to ask him to take such a big risk.

She stared at the trowel. She wished it were a magic wand that she could wave to make his life perfect.

Her nostrils flared and she glared at the far corner of the garden. More than anything, though, she wanted to find him and beg him to dig deep and find the courage to fall in love with her.

She forced herself to her feet. *Not going to happen.* She had more self-respect than that. She shouldn't have to beg anyone to love her. Blake had made his decision. His choices were his responsibility, not hers.

All she could do now was move forward with her life and make plans for the future. Good plans. She'd spend time with the people who did love her—her friends here in Callenbrook—and when she went off to university next year, she'd make new friends.

Dragging in a breath, she nodded. She *could* do this.

She started to bend down when a sixth sense had her nape prickling. Turning, she found the man who'd preoccupied her thoughts standing on Iris's back veranda. He vaulted the fence and strode towards her, stopping several feet away. 'Hello, Nina.'

She stared—she probably gaped—and clocked the turbulence in his eyes. She had to plant her feet to stop herself from throwing herself into his arms. *Self-respect.*

Closing her eyes briefly, she nodded and swallowed. 'The thing I said about Christmas… I only meant for this Christmas, Blake, not for all Christmases.'

She'd give him that much reassurance. Perhaps it would help him find the peace he needed to move forward, because a war raged in those heartbreakingly Mediterranean-blue eyes of his, and she hated that she'd caused it. He might not be able to love her, but she didn't want him whipping himself with guilt and regret. She didn't want him miserable. She wanted him to be happy and at peace.

For some reason her words had him huffing out a laugh. Closing his eyes, he lifted his face to the sun. She gazed hungrily at that beautiful face. The Christmas after next…? A year and a couple of months. It'd give her something to aim for—a timeframe to put herself back together again. She could do that, couldn't she?

'I've been dreaming of your voice, Nina.' Those eyes speared hers. '*Literally* dreaming. When I wake up and realise it's a dream, I'm gutted. But the actual reality of your voice is a hundred times more potent than the dream.'

Her heart surged against her ribs. She told it to stop being stupid. Blake wasn't telling her this in a loverlike way. He was simply in a panic because he'd lost his grandmother and best friend in what had to feel like one fell swoop and… She swallowed. And that was hard going for anyone.

She didn't want to make his life dark and difficult, but she couldn't perform miracles either. She'd hold out the promise of Christmas next year, and maybe it'd give him some comfort.

'So Christmas next year. In London. Sounds fun, right? So if that's what you came to check…'

'It's not.'

She folded her arms. Tight. Ignored the burning at the backs of her eyes. 'What are you doing here, then, Blake?'

'You only gave me until Corfu to get my head together, to work out how I felt about your…revelation.'

Bombshell more like, but she refrained from correcting him.

Those beautiful eyes turned rueful. 'It wasn't long enough. Mind you, maybe I needed the shock of seeing you walk away for me to finally work out the truth.' He held her gaze. 'You were right— or, at least, almost right—when you told me I was half in love with you. You always could read me like a book. The thing is, I'm not just half in love with you, Nina. I'm completely in love with you.'

She remained as motionless and still as if they were playing a game of Statues—she didn't jump for joy—and he frowned. 'I thought…' His Adam's apple bobbed. 'I thought that's what you wanted to hear.'

'Until you told me in Corfu that if heartbreak was the price you had to pay to protect your lone-wolf status, then you'd be willing to pay it. In what world do you think it would make me happy to know you're as miserable as me?'

He let out his breath on a whoosh, his shoulders losing their hard edges. 'But I was wrong. I was stupid. I didn't know then that letting you walk away was the biggest hurt I could ever inflict upon myself.'

She unfolded her arms to press her hands to her ears and block out his words. 'Look, Blake, I know you're panicking about losing your best friend but—'

Seizing her hands, he pulled them away. 'And why am I panicking, Nina? Because losing my best friend means losing the best part of my heart.'

He dragged one of her hands to his chest and held it there. His heart pounded against her palm, strong and steady.

'I've been off balance since August when I saw you in the flesh for the first time in ten years—because not only were you the girl who'd been my main support throughout my entire life, but you were also a beautiful woman that I wanted with a hunger I'd never experienced before.'

Wait. What? *Really...?*

'The mistake was thinking those two things were at odds instead of the perfect combination.'

Her mouth worked, but words refused to come. Was he saying he *would* let love into his life? Was he saying that he would risk loving *her*?

'The thing is, you've always been in my inner circle. When I spoke about being a lone wolf and not trusting anyone with my heart, that referred to everyone outside that inner circle. It didn't apply to Gran and it didn't apply to you. Because I already knew the quality of your hearts, you see, knew you could be trusted. And your heart, Nina...your heart is solid gold.'

Despite her best intentions, her stomach fluttered and her heart lifted. She couldn't seem to catch her breath. 'Why didn't you tell me this back in Corfu?'

'Because I hadn't worked it out yet. You walked away and I was...lost. I traipsed the streets around the harbour until I was exhausted and eventually threw myself down on the bench. An old man was sitting there and he recognised the source of my *agitation*.'

A half-rueful, half-humorous smile played across his lips, and the darkness inside her lightened to a grey mist that started to dissolve in the sun.

'He asked about the lady who had me tied up in such knots and when I told him you were my best friend, and that I could no longer think straight around you because you were so beautiful, he laughed and told me that was the best.'

'The best?' she echoed.

'Because I already knew the quality of your heart—your soul—which meant I'd be able to trust you with all of myself.'

The phrase made her catch her breath. *The quality of her heart.*

'And that the rest was a beautiful bonus.'

A beautiful bonus? Was that how Blake really saw it?

He widened his stance. 'You've accused me in the past of complicating things, and you're right. I could only see how love had the potential to sabotage my life rather than the source of strength it could be. I've spent all this time worrying that giving into our attraction meant risking our friendship. I could only see the dangers. What I never thought to consider, Nina, was all I'd be gaining—and that what was happening between us was a natural and exciting evolution of our relationship.'

She tried to grab hold of her heart before it took off in flight. Did he *really* mean that?

'And I realised that turning my back on that to maintain my lone-wolf status would hurt me in ways I'd never imagined before. It would make me cold and hard, leave me lonely and far poorer in all the essentials that make a person worthy, and make life worthwhile.'

She couldn't do anything but stare.

'If I wanted to remain true to myself, if I wanted to live in a way that made me proud—in a way that was the antithesis of my parents' lives—then I needed to trust in that evolution. From friends...' his lips twisted '...and because of my misplaced pride, to enemies—'

'You were *never* my enemy.'

'To friends again, but not like before. Because I wanted you, and I could see you wanted me too. So, friends with an edge.'

Okay, that was a fair call.

'To lovers.'

Their eyes caught and held. What a lover Blake had proved to be too—tender, gentle, demanding, playful, encouraging, generous. Her mouth dried. And satisfying. *Very* satisfying. Fingernails dug into her palms as heat rippled through her. He'd taken her to heights she hadn't known existed, had unleashed things inside her she hadn't known she'd been capable of.

'With you I learned the difference between making love and sex. I didn't want to question that too closely or analyse it too deeply, afraid of what I'd find. Which is that I'd fallen hopelessly in love with you.'

He looked utterly discombobulated and her heart became a puddle of warmth in her chest. He *loved* her. He really, truly *loved* her. And he was going to take a risk on them. If she had a half-decent singing voice she might've broken into song—like a Disney movie.

He thrust out his jaw. 'The thing is it doesn't have to be *hopelessly* in love. You and I aren't ever going to play out my parents' relationship.'

'I'm not manipulative like your mother.'

Reaching out, he touched her cheek. 'And neither am I.'

She sucked in a breath and pressed her hand over that generous heart of his. 'You're not.'

'And we're both stronger people than our fathers.'

'Absolutely.'

'Which means we can love each other *and* remain true to our individual moral codes.' He said the words as if they were a revelation. His hands curved around her shoulders. 'And, Nina, that means we can fall in love *hopefully*. There's nothing hopeless about it.'

'Nothing hopeless about it at all,' she whispered. She had to reach up on tiptoe then and kiss him. He kissed her back with such an aching hunger all she could do was cling to him as it swept her along.

Lifting her in his arms, he strode to the veranda and settled in her electric-blue chair, nestling her in his lap. He kept one arm firmly around her waist, with the other he gently pushed the hair from her face. 'I love you, Nina. And that doesn't even scare me. It feels like a miracle.' He shrugged. 'My heart belongs to you. It always did.'

She turned her cheek into his palm and kissed it. 'I love you, Blake. I mean, I've always loved you and you've always been the best time I've ever had.'

One side of his mouth kicked up and his chest puffed out and he looked so ridiculously happy she wanted to laugh. She didn't. She had more to say yet.

'I love you in a different way now, though. A deeper way, a fuller way…an exciting way. I didn't know love could be like this.'

Blue eyes flared. 'Like being at home and being on an adventure at the same time?'

Exactly! She grinned. 'Like being on a Mediterranean holiday.'

He laughed. 'Want to spend Christmas in the Mediterranean?'

She laughed then too, because she had so much happiness lifting through her. 'I think you should buy a house in Portofino.' Then they could sneak out for skinny-dipping adventures in the dark of the night whenever they wanted.

'Or a yacht.'

'Nice idea!'

He settled her more securely on his lap. 'I gave our immediate future some thought on the flight here. The thing is you love Callenbrook, so I was thinking I could move back here and we could turn your two duplexes into one home big enough for the family we'll hopefully eventually have. After you've finished your university degree, of course.'

She stared. He'd move back to Callenbrook? For her? If there'd been a doubt in her mind about the sincerity of his love, it would've fled now. 'Blake, I...'

'I mean, you did say you wanted kids eventually and, well... It seems amazing—a miracle—that *that* life has become a possibility for me.'

She touched his cheek. 'Are you sure? What about your work, your company?'

'I have people to run the company for me. I don't like the wheeling and dealing. I like building things, making things...and there's a computer game that's unfolding in my mind that I'd like the chance to develop. And seriously, Nina, I can do that anywhere.' One broad shoulder lifted. 'So where better than in this place that you love? I used to love it too, before all of the bad things happened.' He grew serious. 'With you at my side, I know I could love it again.'

Her heart broke free of her body to soar in joyous circles. She threw her arms around his neck and hugged him. 'I love you, Blake.' She eased away. 'I love you completely and utterly.'

Their kiss was a promise and it felt like freedom and family and fun. Mostly, though, it felt like love. They didn't come up for air for a very long time, too intent on showing the other how much they were loved, intent on soothing the hurts of the last few days, and promising each other a future they could cherish.

When he finally lifted his head, they were both breathing hard. 'Will you teach me to line dance?'

'Just try and stop me.' She stuck her nose in the air. 'And just wait and see. You'll love it.'

He grinned, and then he started to laugh and she thought it might be her new favourite sound in the world. 'I don't doubt it. And will you also marry me and make me the happiest man alive?'

She cocked her head to the side and pretended to consider it. 'Okay, but only if I can have the Deadly Sins as my maids of honour.'

'Perfect!'

This time when they kissed, they didn't stop.

* * * * *

If you enjoyed this story, check out these other great reads from Michelle Douglas

Secret Fling with the Billionaire
Tempted by Her Greek Island Bodyguard
Claiming His Billion-Dollar Bride
Accidentally Waking Up Married

All available now!

Get up to 4 Free Books!

**We'll send you 2 free books from each series you try
PLUS a free Mystery Gift.**

Both the **Harlequin® Historical** and **Harlequin® Romance** series feature
compelling novels filled with emotion and simmering romance.

YES! Please send me 2 FREE novels from the Harlequin Historical or Harlequin Romance series and my FREE Mystery Gift (gift is worth about $10 retail). After receiving them, if I don't wish to receive any more books, I can return the shipping statement marked "cancel." If I don't cancel, I will receive 5 brand-new Harlequin Historical books every month and be billed just $6.39 each in the U.S. or $7.19 each in Canada, or 4 brand-new Harlequin Romance Larger-Print books every month and be billed just $7.19 each in the U.S. or $7.99 each in Canada, a savings of 20% off the cover price. It's quite a bargain! Shipping and handling is just 50¢ per book in the U.S. and $1.25 per book in Canada.* I understand that accepting the 2 free books and gift places me under no obligation to buy anything. I can always return a shipment and cancel at any time by calling the number below. The free books and gift are mine to keep no matter what I decide.

Choose one: ☐ **Harlequin Historical** (246/349 BPA G36Y)   ☐ **Harlequin Romance Larger-Print** (119/319 BPA G36Y)   ☐ **Or Try Both!** (246/349 & 119/319 BPA G36Z)

Name (please print)

Address   Apt. #

City   State/Province   Zip/Postal Code

Email: Please check this box ☐ if you would like to receive newsletters and promotional emails from Harlequin Enterprises ULC and its affiliates. You can unsubscribe anytime.

Mail to the Harlequin Reader Service:
IN U.S.A.: P.O. Box 1341, Buffalo, NY 14240-8531
IN CANADA: P.O. Box 603, Fort Erie, Ontario L2A 5X3

Want to explore our other series or interested in ebooks? **Visit www.ReaderService.com or call 1-800-873-8635.**

*Terms and prices subject to change without notice. Prices do not include sales taxes, which will be charged (if applicable) based on your state or country of residence. Canadian residents will be charged applicable taxes. Offer not valid in Quebec. This offer is limited to one order per household. Books received may not be as shown. Not valid for current subscribers to the Harlequin Historical or Harlequin Romance series. All orders subject to approval. Credit or debit balances in a customer's account(s) may be offset by any other outstanding balance owed by or to the customer. Please allow 4 to 6 weeks for delivery. Offer available while quantities last.

Your Privacy—Your information is being collected by Harlequin Enterprises ULC, operating as Harlequin Reader Service. For a complete summary of the information we collect, how we use this information and to whom it is disclosed, please visit our privacy notice located at https://corporate.harlequin.com/privacy-notice. Notice to California Residents – Under California law, you have specific rights to control and access your data. For more information on these rights and how to exercise them, visit https://corporate.harlequin.com/california-privacy. For additional information for residents of other U.S. states that provide their residents with certain rights with respect to personal data, visit https://corporate.harlequin.com/other-state-residents-privacy-rights/.

HHHRLP25